FAERIEME

FAERIEME

The Universe Awakens

T.F. Burks

To order additional copies of this book, contact:
Xlibris
1-888-795-4274
www.Xlibris.com
Orders@Xlibris.com
721914

CONTENTS

CHAPTER 1

Discovery

As I slept that evening, I was still plagued by the tugging feeling I had been having all my life. I've always had memories of a person that I had never met or seen. It's like a haunting feeling of something or someone always around you that you cannot see. You dream about them, and through dreaming, you are discovering who they are to you. I found myself looking for him in every person I met. It didn't matter how old I was, and I was very young when the dreams began. They were haunting memories of a man whose soul I knew I would run into again in this life. I longed to see him again. Dreaming about him was not enough. I wanted more—no, I needed more—and this was the curse that I had been plagued with for as long as I could remember. Thoughts ran through my head that evening before I slept, unable to turn my thoughts off, unable to rest my mind and my soul.

Do I know him already, will I ever meet him, and does this person really even exist?

The next day I woke as normal, going through the motions of my old, boring routine. Then it was off to my new job; a new adventure awaited me somehow. I felt excited that finally I had reached my goal (as small as it was).

I was working for the hospital I thought was the best in the country. I had always wanted to work there, doing what I had practically fallen into once upon a time long ago. This place called to me all my life. I couldn't explain it. I just knew it was where I needed to be, and no matter what it took, I was going to end up at that institution. Finally, my persistence paid off, and I was on my way into the unknown part of my future. Herein my story lies.

You see, I live in a sleepy small beach town that's in the lovely state of California near Santa Cruz. Santa Cruz, unusually, is infamous for its underground alternative/vampire scene and other things. Not very many people know this, and why should they? Most people will just think it's a typical beach tourist town with a boardwalk, some cool rides, and great surf. I, however, have lived in this area all my life and learned of this over the years.

My home is quaint and unique; it seems to attract artists and musicians and mostly some oddly behaved, shunned-by-society folk as well. I've always loved being a part of a place that connects itself through art and music, as it makes for a better connection with people no matter who or what they may be.

I am an only child, and I loved the time that I had to myself to think and appreciate the moments, for as we grow older, often this existence steals those moments away from us like a thief in the night. I can remember playing outside, thinking of the great big world all around me. I would climb my favorite tree in the backyard during dusk and sing to my heart's content. I loved this time and space that I had. I suppose this was the very beginning of learning how to meditate. No matter how bad I felt or how angry everyone around me seemed, I had always felt love and peace in the afternoon sunlight, butterflies flitting around me, and dragonflies dancing in the last bit of sunshine. All these moments were sacred to me, and I wanted to learn more about them. I wanted to understand the immortal soul and where it came from. Did it transcend time and space? Did the god I was made to understand and believe in create this energy that makes us who we are to live again and again and meet up with the same souls over and over? Is this where my dreams come from, soul memories? Of course, I asked myself if there was a master plan for me. I would ask this and wonder, because it seemed as though I was unwanted and different. I longed for understanding. I would often want to give up on myself, giving into the actions of others that made me feel like I was useless and a waste of time. This was family. So I chose to forge my own way and look for the souls from long ago.

We often wonder where our personal gifts come from, and I always seemed different from the rest of my family. It was of great comfort to be able to breathe in the afternoon air and feel that you are one with the universe. Every so often, I would see a glimpse of something familiar, but it always seemed that it was fleeting and short-lived.

Like pictures in a scrapbook, I would have glimpses into what I thought to be my imagination, not having any idea that any of it could be real. I would imagine great worlds—beautiful and rich with life, vibrant. In those worlds, there were different types of beings. Some had wings, and some looked like insects mixed with people. Some were so mesmerizingly beautiful that I wished I was one of them, and I would pray every single day and night that I was or that I could be taken from where I was and brought to the place of my dreams.

Time is a funny thing; it keeps moving forward regardless of if we are ready for it to move or not. Time is cruel, and so are most people, but here I am in this life. What was I to do? I continued to dream of great things—going to college and becoming someone of great importance to this society—and so I focused very hard to make it to the place I thought I would be in this life. However, it seemed there was another path I would journey on.

This was what I found to be cruel about life. I felt as though I would be standing, looking at a road that was clear for me to go down. The road was paved, and I could see ahead. However, once I started down one path, there would be a roadblock, and then another. Eventually, I would have to choose another road, and that road would be harder and more weathered. Again I would come across something sinister lurking in the darkness of my life, preventing me from moving forward. I couldn't figure it out. *Why me?* I would ask. *Why is it so easy for everyone else, but when it comes to me, my road has turned into a dead end?* It seemed to be a test of faith, perhaps, or endurance or both. All I knew was that I kept moving forward and believing that there was a grand plan and I must continue even though I felt as if I couldn't. This new job I recently got was my new hope, and I was excited again. I could feel my heart warming up again.

Since I was hired into my new job, I knew there would be a substantial commute! I drove a great car, and I knew it would help me get to where I needed to be. I felt as though this silly little car was alive somehow and at times knew that it belonged just to me. It totally fit my personality perfectly, sassy and fun! This was how I dealt with the sacrifice of time spent on the road. I had to try to make it fun; it was part of the grand scheme. I know I've been blessed to have certain items or animals in my life who find their way to me, but there was a certain event in particular that was something special. She was my guardian and a warm comfort of my soul. I was never lucky enough to have the animal I needed growing up. My family was strange about these things and found them to be more trouble than a gift. I never truly understood how they made the decisions they did, but I know now how those decisions affected me. It was as if I was an afterthought, a close second to everything else. My little guardian is named Bella. She is a beautiful kitty that found her way to me. She is what is known as a fairy eared cat. A very rare female orange tabby. My little protector, and my little friend.

My life seemed like every other child's life that consisted of school, studying, and doing chores. Like everyone else I would look forward to Easter baskets from the Easter Bunny, Christmas, and birthdays. Although I was never allowed to be with other children, sure, I went to public school, but when I was invited to go play, my family wouldn't have it. I was very lonely and very confused. There were no trips to Disneyland, or the park, no family vacations. I imagine my family had their reasons, since I seemed to be the "odd" child. What I neglected to mention is that when I was quite young and used to play outside, A LOT. I would be surrounded by an unusual number of dragonflies, butterflies, frogs, bluebirds, and hummingbirds. I thought that this was normal. Apparently, it wasn't, and I felt punished for it. I was sensitive to everything and would see things others could not. This was my life, and it was all that I knew. I'm sure my family was terrified that I might share this unusual information with people, and then what? So as I grew, I learned that life wasn't that nice, nor was it fair, but I survived it and proceeded to grow up with the feeling weighing heavy in my heart that some big part of me was missing, always missing.

Time kept marching on and on, and I was married at twenty-one years of age. I thought this was what was supposed to happen. I believed in Prince Charming and love at first sight, so why not me, right? Let's just say he was never Prince Charming and that the age of twenty-one is not an age to make any major life decisions. Both such decisions were terribly wrong for me. I was desperate to figure out what was missing in my world, and I had hoped this man would fill that void. Everything else seemed to fall apart on me, so I tried to build a castle with a handful of sand, my soul so desperate to find its story. The only thing I did know with conviction was that I was to have a child, a boy, to be exact. The child was not to be with the first husband. He was a very confused and bitter person that had no interest or concern for me as a human being. Needless to say, after the beatings, and verbal abuse that marriage ended. His parents begging me to leave him because they knew the type of broken person he truly was. Now the second man in my life had come along, trying to "rescue me" I knew deep down it was a disaster, but I also knew that he would be the father of my son, as I was not able to become pregnant and keep a child with anyone else. He was what I'd like to think of as "the sperm donor", the only thing that mattered, or that was worth anything that came from that man was his sperm donation. Unfortunately he was worse than the first! The utter evil that lurked inside of him seemed to be dark and cruel, almost demonic in nature. None of that seemed to matter though. I was to have a child and his DNA was willing and able. It wasn't always all bad, as there were times that he was fascinating to talk to. He was a plethora of information. This information that he would share from time to time seemed to be what I needed to hear and learn. So I made that best of a less than ideal situation. It was a dangerous situation, and my both my son's life and my own were threatened on several occasions. Once again I had nowhere to go, and no one to go to, but now I have this little person I need to keep safe and take care of.

I became very aware of my surroundings at a very young age, and I had the strangest memories that to this day have never left me. I had to learn to catalog these "soul memories," as I call them, in my own mind just to make sense of my existence. I also learned that I could not trust my family with these unusual memories that haunted me, along with my strange dreams and little visitors when I was a very small child. I learned I could not trust them with much, especially my heart. If I had told them, I am certain I would have been placed in a mental hospital somewhere and heavily medicated. Don't get me wrong. All these thoughts and all these memories didn't make me extra special, just constantly confused, and estranged from the people in my life that were supposed to matter.

In light of this epiphany of mine, I then tried to understand the human condition. In other words, why do bad things continue to happen to certain people who seem to not deserve it? But then the question is, who am I to decide who deserves what on this earth, even myself? I am unable to call time a friend, but the universe did give me my son. The marriage to his father was an abusive, horrible mess number 2, and I was beginning to accept the possibility that I was not deserving of a *good life*. So I continued on trying to be the best mommy that I could be to my son, even though I felt like a total failure at all other things in my life.

Three years went by so quickly, and I was not remembering who I was. All I knew was that I needed to be on my own again with my little boy and try to become who I needed to be, whatever that was. After the loaded gun being pushed into my left temple and my life being threatened in front of my 24 month old son, I had to find a place to go. It was a miracle as to how I was able to calmly talk my way out of such a situation, and keep my son safe. I had to beg my mother to let my son and I stay with her. It was difficult for me, and my pride was compromised, but I had another person besides myself to think of and he came first. My mother was kind enough to agree, and at first she was kind of excided to have us there, but we were two very different people and the living situation always seemed strained. Our living situation continued to be a challenge. I was still young enough to meet someone and start over for a third time, and I continued to be hopeful. Soon I met my third husband, a sweet and gentle man, but very immersed in this human world, with no concept of anything else. He had no wants or needs spiritually or otherwise. They all seemed to be earthly essentials for a *normal life*, and I needed that "normal" in my life as well. I had to try to push back the feelings of something missing and something more. I had to stop remembering things that were only dreams and that I was crazy for thinking of them. Our life began to get rocky, but our life began nonetheless! I was soon to start a very important time in my life that included this, and the new job, but I digress.

As I woke that morning and got ready for my new job, I had an element of excitement and fear—fear of the unknown, fear that represented the culmination of my total existence—and I wondered if the people there would be professional and like me at all on a personal level. I am a laboratory technician. I wanted to be a research scientist (MD/PhD) but never quite made it. I liked what I did for a living since it was so very close to what my heart truly desired and wanted to do. I had this insane idea that I would be the individual to find the cause and cure for cancer, having had a premonition as a young child that my beloved grandparents would die from this horrible manifestation of a disease.

It was surreal as I drove up to the hospital that day and parked my car. I walked in, very unsure of myself, and put on my cheery, happy-go-lucky personality.

As I did my walk through the lab, there seemed to be so many faces, and it was a bit overwhelming, really. So with my head down and in deep thought, I approached a common area where there were about four people working, and a truly unexpected thing happened to me at that moment. Two doctors sat at computers, and two other people buzzed around them, performing their usual duties. All at once my head rose, and there he was—white lab coat, dark hair, stunning smile. He was amazing, and he captivated me all at once. He was too perfect, everything I could remember from those plaguing dreams. I stopped in my tracks at once, not even realizing that I had been staring intently at this new individual, this doctor now standing before me.

Immediately I looked at his left hand for a ring (an old habit).

Oh, please let him be single, I said to myself. No ring was present. *Excellent! Now for a look into those eyes. The eyes being the window to the soul. What color could they be? Who is this person, and why is this happening to me now so late in the game of my life?* I have recognized too many souls in this life, and I could not risk making more mistakes. Risking what little bit of normal I had built into my life.

He seemed to stop in his tracks as well and looked toward me. Our eyes met, and time seemed to stand still. His eyes were hazel with mostly green specks, and they peeked at me through long, thick dark eyelashes. He was so beautiful, more beautiful than he needed to be to me, and I wondered if anyone else was able to see what I was seeing. Those sixty seconds seemed eternal as we stared into each other's eyes. I wondered if he was feeling the same as I was in that exact moment, and I wondered what he was thinking. All at once the spell seemed to unfortunately be broken with the sound of commotion and a phone frantically ringing. I tried to shake this new feeling off but couldn't help but stare continually at someone that seemed so unfairly familiar to me.

I couldn't stop looking at him as if I knew him from somewhere, somehow, long ago, but how?

There he is, I thought to myself. *Now what?*

Was this whom I had been dreaming about all my life, really? I felt transported to an earlier time in my life, when I was single and things seemed simpler for me, and all that was usually on my mind was this reoccurring dream. It became a part of me, like breathing. At some point, it was a comforting thing, when things in life became complicated and virtually intolerable.

This man was so familiar to me. Who could he be, and why in that moment did I feel so attracted to him? When those sixty seconds finally ended, I felt a sense of guilt coupled with wonder. I felt robbed of time spent with him. In that small space in time, I imagined our lives together, him holding me tightly to him and staring into my eyes with just as much fascination as I had for him. I wondered of how and why things seemed to have such poor timing in my life, never seeming to be in the right place at the right time. Yet there he stood, trying ever so hard to be polite. He tilted his head toward me and forced an awkward but spectacular smile. The look on his face was unmistakable that he might have had the same exact experience as I had. I thought to myself, *I am married, and I love my husband, so how can this be?* Reality quickly set in again as I tried to gather myself back together, realizing my surroundings and my current predicament. All space and time seemed to stop in those sixty seconds. The air around me did not move, and I felt transported. This is why I had to gather myself. It was a feeling of dropping a handful of small items and having to carefully pick them all up and account for every last piece.

Now, I had always considered myself a philosopher by my own right, constantly contemplating the reasons for my own existence and what purpose I had on this earth. My name is Titania Folklund, an odd name, yes, but no one could ever really explain why they decided to name me this. I had always been regarded by others as pretty, I guess, or striking, although I never actually felt that way about myself. I am a dark-haired brunette (my hair almost black in color) with golden-honey eyes, olive skin, and a petite frame. My husband teases me about how little and fragile he thinks I am. People I really don't know tend to stop me to tell me how pretty they think I am, and it is just an uncomfortable feeling because I never felt special in this world. It's really kind of strange because I don't have the same opinion about myself. Self image issues. This is something I have had to deal with my whole life, so it became routine. I almost expected it. People and/or friends would try to be nice and compliment me, which was great, but then there was always that struggle inside myself to try to believe them. That is what I expected, the struggle to believe the nice things every day, and to be thankful for what I have.

Life had truly taken its toll on me, and I was tired. I had developed a saying that I would repeat to myself. I would say that my soul was tired, because I felt okay really, but my soul, my spirit felt ancient (burdened really). I was so weary and jaded in the life that I was in. I was exhausted with trying to understand the people and environments that surrounded me. People seemed cruel and selfish, and life was complicated more so for me than anyone I had ever encountered in my life. New events were about to complicate things even more so now than ever. I wondered if this was something that I had done to myself. Was it karma, and what is karma exactly? How does it all work? What could I have done in this life or the others? Life seemed to blow me in every direction, and I could feel the emotions of everything and everyone around me. Sometimes I was able to feel the burdens of the world upon my shoulders and wonder if this was the way God felt sometimes (having been raised as a Roman Catholic).

Even as a child, I seemed like a bee without a hive. Sure I was smart and somewhat driven, but life had a different plan in store for me, it seemed. The trick is realizing what your meant to do. My mother did not seem like my mother. She didn't really know me the way I would have liked, and my father and uncles had no interest in me at all as a person. Everyone seemed to run in the opposite direction. They were all so involved in their own life and existence. I suppose they were all trying to find their own way and I was in the way of that. Didn't help that I was weird to them. My life did not seem like my life, but I tried to deal with what I had and tried to make the best of what seemed to be many poor situations. All my life I have been fascinated with the theory of other dimensions, or other worlds. I would imagine that perhaps in another dimension I was successful and beautiful and respected, or I was still a little girl with a mother and a father who were so proud of me and loved me more than anything. I started to take my thoughts further and imagine that if there were other dimensions, there could be other beings within these dimensions as well and places within places of an infinite universe.

While I was growing up, I thought I was seeing fairies at dusk and through the night. They were comforting and silent. They would help me try to fall asleep. I've always had trouble with trying to sleep. My brain doesn't seem to want to rest, so I would pray for some peace. I kept this information to myself mostly. I can remember as far back as not being able to walk yet and thinking as I stood at our screen door how wonderful nature was. I remember ladybugs and butterflies landing on the screen as if watching me with as much amazement as I had for them. This was my time growing up to get close to nature and understand the universe. This was what I thought and believed, and I felt something speaking to me in every moment of my day back then, and I miss those days. I had so many aspirations of who and what I'd become, and I was excited to be alive when I was young. This is what my family did not understand about me. It was as if I were from another place and time, and they couldn't quite get me, or they really didn't want to.

I felt drawn to certain things in my life, and part of that feeling was being able to experience as many religions as I could. They all fascinated me, and I was determined to learn them all. I worked so very hard toward my personal goals, or what I thought were my goals, but all my goals seemed to be set in vain, and my future plans were broken into pieces by various challenges, circumstances, and people, yet I still had strong feelings of hope that remained deep within me somehow. The word *hope*—therein lies a multidimensional word. No matter how hard you try to describe the word *hope*, in essence, it is an indescribable feeling that comes from what I like to think of as a burning ember. It may not be a fire, but it can glow hot for long periods and then dim until you feel it has nearly burned itself out. It is reaching those goals and seeing those small miracles everyday that can turn that ember into a fire.

Despite all my failed efforts in relationships and two marriages later, I remained a loving and hopeful person. I was giving up on all humans! They seemed cruel and uncaring. I couldn't begin to explain to you how I could have remained hopeful, but there seemed to be something continually protecting my spirit and that ember I spoke of earlier. All along, my dreams continued, dreams of this Other World that I lived in while I slept, and the one individual that seemed to haunt me always. He was intriguing and wonderful and, from what I had learned from him, felt more like a home I longed to know. I loved him while I was there, and I am sure he loved me too. I felt as if he did. Our life in this dream world was delightful, and I was only able to taste of it on occasion, and it was delicious. The experiences were so familiar, like an old friend but more. If one could even imagine trying to put your best friend, mother, father, grandparents, confidant, someone whom you respect and look up to, and your lover, it would be the person that haunted my dreams. Any kind of meaning of the word *love*—this is what I felt while in those dreams. They were a wonderful escape from the wicked world I was born into, and most nights I did not want to awaken.

While growing up, I aspired to be in the medical field as a physician. I worked very hard in school toward this goal. I had to prove to myself that I could accomplish this goal and become what I thought was an important figure of society. I wanted to help people somehow, but once the time came and the scholarships appeared in the mail or joining an armed force, they were quickly intercepted by family members dispelling any hopes of higher education and life progress. My mother, for example, was always incredibly frightened of losing anything that belonged to her, whether that be time, money, or me.

No matter what I did, I was not able to reach any of my goals. There always seemed more pressing things to do, such as get a job, help out with bills, and pay my own way even while still living at home. This was thought to make me a responsible adult somehow, and I suppose that it ultimately did. Those responsibilities always took precedence over school or anything that seemed to be important to me. Then it became more pressing to just get out of the house! Still I did what my family thought was the right thing to do. My mother wasn't a bad person that wanted to see me suffer; she actually wanted to see me succeed, but only as a survivor like she was, because that was all she knew how to be. My mother had her own bad times in her life and had found the missing piece of her heart. Good or bad, she did everything she could to hold on to it and not let it go. That meant a lot of sacrifice of family, and very personal beliefs that she had within her very soul had now been compromised for this love she had. For the most part, she did not understand what it was that I needed out of this life or what my soul needed out of this life to feel complete. My mother and I had never seemed to agree on anything. There were so many occasions, I felt disappointed and displaced, as if I were from another dimension or something. When I spoke, it seemed that no one was able to understand what it was I was trying to convey at that moment. My mother seemed to be the most confused of all, and the rest of the family just ignored me as if I were a ghost to them. It is a strange thing to say that I loved my mother like a daughter, and I always wanted the best for her and I tried to tolerate the tantrums of frustration that came with having a mother, or entire family for that matter, with a younger soul than me. I had always felt, and I believe everyone in my family believed, that our roles were reversed. She was so young at this life and quite enjoyed her earthly plane. She would often yell and argue that she was the mother and I was the daughter! Such a strange argument to have with a two-year-old little girl. My mother reminded me of a child in a great big toy store—overwhelmed at times but excited to be there, always wanting whatever it was that she saw, and mad when she couldn't get her way, but always happy to be inside the toy store.

Yes, I feel I am an older soul, and I have no explanation for this feeling. It's just something that I knew to be true.

There seemed to always be something in my way in this life: a poor math teacher that held my chances of going to the right college in the palm of his hands and chose to toss my future away as if it were a piece of trash to him, an inexperienced young mother, an alcoholic father who didn't want me, a stepfather that had a whole mess of his own problems that he couldn't deal with properly. Perhaps it was just bad timing coming into this world, I suppose. Always wrong place wrong time. I have experienced a broken home, abandonment, and loss of money, time, and family. It seemed as though I was on my own, and I was the only child. I just woke up one day and decided that I could not take another day of living the way that I had been for the past six years at my mother's house. I was not a part of the new life she had found for herself, and I knew that. A painful reality I had to face every day, and always hoping that when I grew up things would just be better. It hurts to be told by your mother that she wished that you were sired by someone else because it would have made her life so much simpler and better, never mind the other problems you had inherited from her decisions, so I packed my bags at eighteen years of age and left. It wasn't her so much as it was the environment as a whole. I did not like where my life was going at all, so I took a big chance and gambled. I had no life there, no childhood, no privacy as it was always invaded. The childhood I did have was robbed from me and I had to save the rest of my spirit. I knew that there had to be more than this I had been experiencing. There had to be something else out there for me besides pain, anger, and constant disappointment. I was not sure what that was, but it couldn't hurt to get out there and discover it. Maybe I had certain expectations that were not met on a consistent basis, but they were the expectations of a child. I had to stop living in the negative thoughts and feelings that I had been drowning in, and where I was living was not the place to be any longer. I always had to keep in the back of my mind the vision of my dreams, and the love within me with the hope that burned like an ember in my soul. It helped me hope for positive changes, and to continue to have my faith in this world that there is indeed something more. I needed to continue to learn how to listen and hear what the voice in my heart was telling me to do.

As I wandered through my teenage years, I had a couple of wonderful boyfriends here and there. One in particular came the closest I had ever come to the love of my dreams.. He reminded me of sunshine hitting the ocean on a summer's eve, and when I was in his presence, I was at peace. After many awkward moments of trying to get his attention, I was victorious and finally had a date. During this whole time, we became pretty good friends. His name was Ian, and he was lovely. I would visit him each day after school where he worked at the ice cream shop on the way home. He was a few years older than I, but he was wonderful. We were only sixteen and fourteen years of age. He finally got the hint that I really liked him, and he asked me to give him my phone number.

"How about I call you? We could grab a burger and a movie. I could call you tomorrow." Ian asked.

I was so happy I must have skipped the rest of the way home.

Nothing could have bothered me that day, but tomorrow never came. The phone never rang, and each time it did, it was a disappointment because it wasn't Ian. Two weeks had passed, and I found myself sulking at school. There was a bit of a buzz about a boy that had been found in a levy near the school. I really didn't pay much attention to the chatter until a newspaper article with a picture found its way to me. Ian, my Ian had died. He was the boy the local police found, my phone number still in his pocket. Our time together would never come, and I was devastated after that. Every day I would walk home from school and stop at the ice cream parlor where he worked. Each day I would daydream, as young girls do, about our lives together. I would dream of being called his girlfriend or meeting his family, and these images made me smile every day and gave me hope. It was lovely to just be able to see his face every day, smiling back at me, and knowing that was such a gift, but now that gift was taken from me and never meant to be. My mother tried to be understanding, but seemed to dismiss my feelings rather quickly saying, "It's not like you were dating him or anything, just get over it!"

Now that real life had me in its clutches, it had a stronghold on me. No fun, just work and hard lessons to learn awaited me. Still I had my soul, my imagination—and hope somehow remained. I looked forward to my slumber where I was able to be at home in my mind. Lost I the world that would create itself as I slumbered. I was always welcome and connected in the land of my dreams where my mystery stranger stood there forever, waiting for me to come home to stay. It was always a peculiar comfort to be in that dream state, his arms always open for me but never seeming to connect with him in the physical. In some of my dreams, I would be alone, searching for him through an ancient meadow. Mist would engulf my feet as I walked barefooted through the moist tall grass in the misty early-morning sunlight. It always seemed that I was searching and never quite found what I was looking for. There were large sequences missing that I absolutely could not remember, and it was frustrating, even in my dreams. He revealed himself to me on his terms always. When I was able to see his face, it was always fuzzy, like someone looking far away at something that wasn't wearing glasses.

It was maddening to wake up each night with him just out of my reach, feeling my heart sink further, deeper into the abyss of my very being, always sad and waiting for something to happen.

While I was growing up, I often had visions and deep-set beliefs that were not typical of a child. I always seemed to know more than the adults that surrounded me—for that matter, more than anyone I ever knew—and it disturbed me. It was frustrating, and sometimes I wished I could just turn it off. It was an ancient knowledge that captivated everyone that encountered me in a very weird way. My mother had not a clue as to what to do with me though. She was not able to relate as a mother.

I could understand why she seemed to have so much trouble.

My mother was a single mother and very much of this earth plane. She finally had decided to leave me with my grandmother and start a new life with a new man. Twelve years passed, as my dreams and visions were lovingly cared for by my gentle grandmother but in a very unusual way. I was not able to speak of my gifts with anyone including my family members (with the exception of my grandmother); they were scary and odd to basic society. After all, who wants to be the misfit? I learned very quickly whom I was able to trust and not trust. No one could know that when I was scared at night, I would see small lights appear that seemed to dance all around me. I was scared at first but got used to these visits, and they helped relax me. Faraway laughter accompanied a beautiful dancing cavalcade above my bed, which softly lulled me to sleep. This was a happy world to me as a child, and I looked forward to my slumber. I would dream of wonderful angels and faeries with the most beautiful faces and was fascinated by their flight of fancy. As the only child, I was not allowed to play with other children, for my grandmother feared that others would find out about my weird little trips and quirks and my special gifts of sight. My grandmother was the only person whom I could be myself around and whom I was able to ask the most obscure questions to. She understood me, possibly even studied me, but was fascinated by me nonetheless.

I knew of things that no one else in my family was familiar with—ancient things and a strange fascination with the Renaissance, as if I had lived in that time, and having never been exposed to the current time that I was in. I recognized sixteenth and seventeenth century art and music at four and five years of age. I felt comfortable reading Shakespeare at a single-digit age. This is a total impossibility due to the fact that the family that I grew up in was in no way interested in the arts of classical music or anything other than the time they lived in. They had no interest in poetry or philosophy, not like I did. I knew the ancient dead language of Latin and could understand it when it was spoken at an early age. I had images of the inner workings of the universe and had a vast knowledge and understanding of religion in general. I knew of ancient places within this world and had no fear of the supernatural. Yes, no fear, because the supernatural always seemed to show itself to me, and I was used to seeing it on a daily basis. It was not a hidden world to me, but unfortunately, there was no one to talk to regarding it. It's not as though I was regarded as the female equivalent of Stephen Hawking; after all, who would ever notice me anyway in that respect (not having a degree to prove my worth in this world)?

As I was coming into my own, I could feel my blood rush through my veins, hot and fierce. My heart beat as that of a rabbit, and soon I learned to control the beating of my heart, slowing it down, breathing deeply, taking in the very essence of what surrounded me. I had always had a perfectly developed sense of smell that no one was able to relate with or understand. Clearly, I kept asking myself, what the heck is going on? Life moved around me in such a way that I seemed to be moving at a faster pace than everything else. I grew to be quite a loving woman, considering everything else that was always up against me. All I had to do was speak, and magic seemed to occur wherever I was. People feared this, and jobs were hard to keep. When people are afraid of something, they tend to push it away and bury it rather than embrace and understand it or simply enjoy what they have encountered and revel in it. As I grew I learned to somewhat wield these gifts, and sometimes even share them with people who needed help. People will always be people and use you until your cup is empty. What most people do not understand is that the universe hears every word you say, but does not know the difference between the good and the bad. So if you are a negative person, always repeating negative thoughts such as, *I will never be successful, or I'm fat,* the universe will continue to give you the things you believe. However, if you believe you are successful and worthy the universe will give you that as well. This is always a difficult thing for people to understand. You make your own rules and the universe is your genie. It may not come right away (which in turn creates doubt), but eventually what you wish usually finds its way to you. It sounds hypocritical of me to say, given the negative thought processes I've had in the beginning of my life. The goal is to understand there is a learning curve and that I finally decided to surrender to this life of mine.

All along life seemed to be blowing me every which way, until I reached what always seemed to be a temporary purpose. As I matured, I discovered there were more people such as myself out there, and this excited me and continued to give me encouragement. I discovered different groups of people and grew comfortable with the more natural religions of the earth. This brought peace to me, and so marks the beginning of my religious studies, but something was missing. Something or someone was always missing. After all the studies and all the experiences, some piece to the puzzle that was my life had disappeared. Simple logic stated that I needed to remain guarded due to some tough life lessons learned in my earlier years of trusting people. The simple truth is that you just can't trust people, and if you do, there are few in this world to trust. People are only human after all and will act as such on a dime! Selfish and antagonistic beings. How could I possibly be one of them? I hated the very thought of it as it made my skin crawl with utter disgust. I disliked the way most of them looked, acted, and smelled, to be perfectly honest, and I had absolutely no idea why. I would often chastise myself for these thoughts.

I tried to find comfort and safety with men and marriage, and after three different attempts and one biological child later, I found that marriage was not what I was searching for at all. I was finding that I was beginning to run out of time. You see, I'm getting older now and beginning to lose touch with what it was I was born with: the knowledge and steadfast knowing of what truly is in this life and not being jaded by society and linear time. Slowly I can feel myself fading in the gifts that I was born with into the background noise until completely evaporating and everything that makes me who I am becoming completely out of my reach.

"I love my husband," I said to my close friend Shawna Stark (who is a witch, by the way).

"I know you do, Titania, but what of your life? Are you happy? Maybe you should just be happy with what it is that you have." Shawna urged.

Shawna was a very important part of my life, as we both discovered that we were truly outside of societal standards in such a way that we actually began to feel who and what we truly were. We both felt not of this world (myself more than Shawna) and that we had so much more to offer this world. We never truly convinced ourselves of actually being supernatural because that would just be weird, right? But we knew we weren't able to just stay in the mainstream. This was an important discovery for me, as I had been practicing a more natural elemental type of religion despite what my family had taught me. I was raised to be a very strict Catholic girl, but I asked too many questions regarding this religion. This perplexed the priests and nuns and made them all feel uneasy when around me as a child. They made me feel evil and not worthy of god's love and sacrifice. This was a cruel thing to do to a child, but then again they are only human right?

As I grew, I was finally able to understand a minute part of my existence here, and that I was able to share this with other people and that was okay if done carefully. The moment of discovery and acceptance was beautiful. It was not until later that I, after this momentous discovery, began to grow even more and ended up moving to a new house in the woods with my third husband and my child Gabriel. For some reason, this house seemed surrounded by what I felt was magical. This was a presence I had not felt since I was a child, and it was a welcome one. It brought comfort to my soul.

CHAPTER 2

Doubt

Life continued on, and I seemed to blossom into a somewhat of a butterfly. Ironically it was my husband John that helped me love myself enough to be beautiful again, but at the same time he was very uncomfortable with this and found this disturbing. My son Gabriel supported me and shared in my visions. Life continued to be difficult though, but I pushed on. As I continued on in my new job, I would see glimpses of my handsome doctor here and there. These encounters were brief at best, and I was able to think of them simply as coincidence or just another handsome guy, but was he? Time passed and quickly turned into a year. I found out that the young doctor's name was Michael and that he was involved with someone, possibly married as well.

All at once, my heart seemed to fall even though I myself was a married woman with children of my own. This was an odd feeling, but again I was able to dismiss it to the back of my mind and move on.

*I am married to a wonderful man, and he is so very kind to m*e, I thought to myself.

Until one day, another young female doctor approached me and asked if I would like to come and work in the intensive care unit of the hospital.

"What are the hours?" I asked.

"I think you would like them. They are 7 a.m. to 3:30 p.m. Would you be interested?" asked the doctor.

"Yes! Sign me up!" I said excited.

"This is not going to be easy, you know. People usually do not want to work in this area because it is too hard," said Robin, who happened to be my boss.

"Are you okay with that?" Robin asked.

"Yes," I answered, unsure myself but willing to grab the position because of the time it would allow me to be able to spend with my family.

Training was soon started, and all seemed to be well. Until one day I came in to find that the young doctor that caught my eye for whatever reason worked in that very department. There he was, big as you please.

Oh, so this is where he has been hiding all this time, interesting, I thought to myself.

He was very shy and didn't speak much, but there was a familiar feel to him that relaxed me. This was not something to really think too deeply about, because after all, we were both married and had children. I often heard stories as Michael would speak to the other doctors about his "lovely, successful wife." The people we worked with all seemed to want to know every small detail of his life, as if they were living through him.

The stories got more and more frequent, and I began to see that perhaps Michael wasn't as happy as everyone so desperately wanted or thought him to be. Not even the pictures he deeply stared into every day, that chronicled every moment of his life seemed to appear empty to him. Every so often, you could see a smile rise from his deep looks from a little picture of a funny moment.

"It is a known fact, Shawna, that when people speak too often of how great their life is, there is typically a problem, wouldn't you agree?" I said adamantly.

"Well, this guy does sound cute. What do you think? Do you like him or something?" Shawna asked.

"No, I don't *like* him, but there is something about him. I just can't pinpoint it," I replied.

I tried to make sense of it all but had to dismiss my thoughts as my life was beginning to crumble around me as usual. What could I do? I married a wonderful man with a less-than-wonderful ex-wife and two children.

My husband's family was very cautious around me and seemed judgemental and scared. This was yet another obstacle for me to try to overcome. I was not able to be myself around these people, and it was stifling, as if being strangled slowly until met by an untimely death. Despite the fact that I was terribly confused about my life and virtual existence, I had to push on with desperate hope of overcoming the evil my husband's ex-wife had cast on my life with this man. There were times I thought I was losing my mind. I couldn't hardly breathe at times totally consumed by the thoughts of the new things I myself allowed in my life. So desperate to be loved and having some stability again. I prayed a lot, and I complained a lot during prayer. I often fought with my own thoughts and feelings. This did not feel normal, and I thought I was crazy. I would think to myself, that perhaps this is what people see when they look at me. Just some crazy woman, that is a hot mess with a wild nature and imagination. Who would want to be around that? I didn't even want to be around myself after having experienced quite possibly the worst person I had ever met in my husband's ex wife. Not to mention my second husband who is probably about as evil and conniving as they come.

"I'm cursed. I'm telling you I'm cursed! I can't seem to shake the bad karma or luck or whatever it is you want to call it. What can I do, or better yet, what have I done to deserve such a life?" I begged out loud while looking up at the sky.

"Is it what I believe in, or have I done something in a past life that was so terrible that I am to be eternally punished in this one? I need answers, some guidance. Please talk to me and help me get through this. I have been through so much, and I am tired. Please, just say something, a sign—anything," I said, still begging out loud as I sat in the meadow just near my home.

Suddenly the wind blew, and the temperature became rather warm. There were no insects, no birds, just silence and an unnatural stillness all around me. In the distance, I could see glimpses of flickering light. As the lights came closer, I could hear voices, small voices almost whispering.

The lights began to buzz around my head and the voices grew louder, but I was unable to see what was in the light. It couldn't have been what I thought it was. *Faeries?*

"Yes," a small voice said, almost angry.

"You know not of who you are or what you are capable of, do you, Titania?"

For the first time in my life, I had heard my name pronounced correctly, and it was beautiful, as if someone had sung a love song.

This can't be real, I thought to myself.

"Reality, here, there, nowhere, who is to say, my dear?" Said the small magical voice.

"Is this my imagination? Are you real? Who and what are you?" I asked fervently.

"I am the wind, I am the water, I am earth, and I am sky. I am speaking to you now, and you ask why? Who and what is it that you think I am, sweet Titania, or do you doubt yourself as you always do once again?" Said the small voice.

"Are you my spirit guide or an angel?" I asked.

"An angel, no, of winged faerie, yes, here to guide you and light the way if you are ready to begin the journey today." The little voice answered.

"Journey, what journey? Are we to go somewhere? I have too many things running through my head, and I am confused. Dare I say I couldn't take another day of second guessing myself and my worth." I replied.

"Oh, dear, don't say that. You are here always for a purpose, and right now, you are to begin your next adventure. I will help you along the way, for my name is Misty. I have been your friend for longer than you can remember now in the state that you are currently in. I have been appointed to see you through this. I am not supposed to be speaking to you as I am, but I couldn't bear to see you cry, and I could feel you hurt no more." Misty replied.

"Misty, what is happening to me in my life now? Why am I so uncomfortable here? My husband has so much negativity around him and this woman." I asked.

"Say no more, for she is also not of this world! She comes from a darker realm, and you have thwarted her. It is said that she has vowed to slowly peck away at you like a terrible artist until you leave her love! It is up to you if you are strong enough to endure this undeserved punishment, or if you have faith in that which it is you seek, you shall find." Said Misty.

With these words, the wind blew, and all life was breathed back into the woods. All was quiet, and Misty had seemingly vanished, I was stunned! The good feelings of my childhood came rushing back into me as if diving into pool.

Still, what did it all mean? Was this my mind playing tricks on me? Am I for sure crazy?

Misty's words haunted me: *"If you have the faith in that which it is you seek, you shall find."*

I had that small tugging feeling once again deep down inside me, but still it was clouded by the events going on in my life. What did this all mean? Could it mean that I had to leave my husband and the life that I had tried to put ten years into, or did it mean that everything was going to be okay?

What is it that I seek? I thought to myself. A truly deep question, indeed. I have never asked myself this question seriously, and if I did, I never did answer it properly.

CHAPTER 3

Rumors

As I arrived at work the next day, I found that I was paired to work with the young married doctor. I was very nervous and a bit clumsy. I felt stupid, like I didn't know what it was that I was doing, even though I had been doing the same job for over ten years now and probably knew more than he did.

What is wrong with me? I wondered.

Somehow I knew he would be there. As I walked through the doors, I could immediately sense him. I paused for a moment as I walked through the last door, eyes closed, breathing as deeply as I could as if to swallow him whole. All this within a fraction of a second, fearing that I would be noticed. Slowly we began to speak to each other, realizing that we liked many of the same things, one of which was music. This was of great significance to me because I often felt that when I found a song and was able to sing it, I could speak directly to the universe, directly to god.. I had the gift of voice as well for some reason. This is what seemed to help me in prayer and communication. Music has always meant so much to me.

I also found that we had the same taste in food, drink, time of day, thought process, etc. It became more and more evident as time wore on that we enjoyed each other's company, although we both remained somewhat guarded. One day while we worked side by side, we had a moment to speak. Michael had many questions for me that had metaphysical undertones. I found this rather surprising as he was a man of science and seemed to be very practical. He spoke of faeries and witches; he asked of groups and clubs and what took place. He wanted my input, and somehow knew that I had this insight. His interest was intense and genuine, and this surprised me greatly. All his questions were answered, and he seemed content. The energy around him seemed to glow, but only I was able to see this and know from where it came, at least I thought I knew. It was very deep inside me and I had an idea that maybe Michael was a part of something else (example, my experience with Misty). As for the others, they became frightened and uncomfortable as Michael and I seemed to grow closer in our friendship.

This was addressed immediately by the other coworkers, and the concern with Michael. I was pulled aside and addressed separately by a peer, and the sting of his words burned deep within me. They were hurtful and mean without merit. We were being accused of having an affair, and rumors began to fly. It was a nightmare. Here Michael was beginning a new promising career, and I thought I had reached my goal, but alas, trouble always seemed to brew inside the minds of small people.

We were both innocent and scared. Michael began to withdraw himself from me, becoming cold and uncomfortably quiet. This hurt me deeply because as I grew to know him, I began to feel a close connection to him, and now this too had ripped this away from me. I could feel the blood within me start to boil, and an ancient anger began to surface unlike any other I had ever felt. This was an unusual feeling. It was not jealousy, nor did I have any evil intentions, I was truly sorrowful. I often wondered if Michael had felt the same. He was not very comfortable speaking to anyone about such things; perhaps he felt a forced guilt. Michael began to act indifferent and cold on a regular basis to me, as if we were strangers that had never spoken to one another. It was as if your own family member began to treat you as a stranger and ignored your very presence. This would hurt anyone terribly, and it hurt me beyond reason. It didn't help that all my life I had felt this way about my own family. They always seemed to prefer to ignore me and pretend I didn't exist, and now it was happening again within the adult world I had created.

As I tried to keep working with him, the glow or aura around him fluctuated, and the colors that surrounded him would change rapidly. I could see that the light that surrounded him depended on whom he worked with and the mood he was in. It was quite difficult for me to read, as it was extremely depressing to be around on a regular basis. My head was so full, and I was unable to understand the immediate moments in time. Rumors flew around, blaming me for a seduction that had never taken place. One coworker treated me as a father would treat his daughter had he been greatly disappointed.

"It's not right, you know," the people at work would say.

"I see the way she looks at him! You should hear her!" They would whisper.

It was terrible and hard to bear. This was a cross I most certainly did not need to carry. Still sometimes Michael would help to calm me (when he was having an unusually normal or brave day), telling me not to listen and that no matter what, he would ultimately do what he wanted, not what others wanted or suggested him to do, and I was torn and confused inside because I wasn't so sure that was the case. This was so confusing, because Michael's actions seemed in the beginning as though he had more than a friendship interest in me, then he would shut down! His words and actions were jumbled and did not make sense. What did his words mean? Was he speaking of us, or remembering another person that meant something to him? I was completely unable to grasp this, as I was so unable to read him properly even though this man seemed like he lived in my soul. Sometimes when one is too close to the situation, one is unable to see what exactly it is that is going on. Situations present themselves and I would easily make the wrong choice. I was blinded by what my heart was telling me. He had been speaking to me in riddles lately, saying something without actually saying anything at all. Each time he found the courage to speak to me, the sentences became more complex to understand, and I felt like a dog running around in circles.

What in the world did he mean, and why can't I understand it? I thought to myself that I had my own life, my own husband, and my own children, who were all forgotten about, overshadowed by the seemingly "perfect" life of Michael.

This was vaguely familiar of a prince and maidservant scenario. The prince is the only one of importance because he seems to have everything. As for the maidservant, the prince is just merely wasting his time. This was the usual behavior of society. Michael was a doctor after all, and I was simply his assistant. Why waste time on "just" an assistant? A doctor would be throwing his whole life away on a simple piece of trash, the people would say, and as the days passed I began to believe those words.

There was a certain déjà vu about the situation that sat so uncomfortably with me. How could my prince allow this? The stars I read spoke to me, saying that we were meant to be a couple. Tarot said we were meant to be a couple, and my heart sang to me in his presence, telling me that we were meant to be a couple, and my soul just knew. How could I be wrong? Furthermore, how could I hurt the people currently in my life? Perhaps in another life or dimension? I reflected on the words spoken by Misty: "If you have the faith in that which it is you seek, you shall find."

The magic within me seemed to grow like a flower, and I could feel it growing inside me, an old knowledge! It was from the pit of a place inside of me so deep, blossoming and exploding, and I did not know how to harness it; I didn't even know what it was. On certain days, strange things would happen. If I thought of something I needed, it would come to me within hours. Coincidence, I thought, but was it? Soon I began to realize the power within me once again. I wanted so badly to control the situation with Michael but was unable to. I could feel him watch me and sensed that he knew me well. Michael always seemed to be inside my head, on the same page, so to speak. How did he know when I was thinking about him? Why was he so tuned into me? It was no accident that we had met, but the question was, for what purpose? I did not want a situation similar to the one I was currently in. I was tired of raising everyone else's children. I wanted to set my own rules and have a little girl of my own, and time was running out! I did not want to cause trouble or destroy another relationship whether it be my own or someone else's. I was tired of having a third party person dictate my life through court orders and a bank account.

This was not my goal! I was guilty, but only of one thing: the romance of loving too much, not just people, but also all things. Situations, life, and the love of what could be—these could be deemed as hope to some. Little did I realize this feeling of loving was part of the old knowledge that lived inside of me for as long as I can remember.

There were many questions: Did I really love Michael, or was it truly my husband whom I loved? Could it be that I had a connection to both men in my life? Michael seemed too frightened to engage in any type of interaction with me. There were only moments here and there with a confused Michael, and it simply was unsettling. What was he afraid of, losing his job, guilt, or just me? I had kissed far too many frogs in my life, but Michael was by far the most handsome, though not yet kissed! Each full moon I would wander into the woods and pray for Misty to speak to me again. I would offer Misty sweet milk and cakes (since this is what the fae people enjoy most). On the fourth full moon, I was doubtful but pushed on with my same plea and sweet treats to offer the fae folk.

Hours passed as I walked aimlessly into the woods alone. As I walked, I looked down at my feet. A bright path was lit by the fair light of the moon. There I was, just wandering slowly in the forest and stepping carefully upon the soft ground until I came upon a faint ring of toadstools mixed with white flower blossoms. I had always heard that this was a forbidden place to come upon and enter into in my studies of the elementals. I contemplated walking away, but my heart pushed me forward. I felt that I had nothing to lose. All at once, I dared to step inside the ring, as if I was gently pulled into a spiral, downward into a beautiful dream. Suddenly, I had disappeared within the ring. I was within the faerie world now, what is known in the old stories as, the Other World! At first I was a bit frightened and found myself alone. I could hear faint sounds in the distance, and the sounds seemed to get closer and closer. Suddenly there they were. Several little beings surrounding me. As they danced and sang around me, I could feel my spirits rise. Time seemed to stand still, and the cold air became warm and inviting. I could hear quick chatter in the breeze. I felt as if I were in a dream. Light sparkled all around as far as I could see and the quickness of the lights all seemed to buzz around me at a rate I had never seen. It was all so frightening and exciting at the same time. Where was I? I thought as I looked about. Then I heard a familiar voice in the distance—it was Misty!

"Glad to see you, Titania, welcome home!" Misty said.

"Home?" I asked. "I am unable to focus, I can just hear you, but nothing else." I replied.

Then softly Misty flew over to me, floating to meet me eye to eye. She was the size of a large bumblebee, small and delicate in stature. She proceeded to raise her small hand and touch my forehead for just a few precious moments, and then Misty removed her touch from me. All at once, the once-hidden world that I could not see became visible to me. There were so many of them staring back at me as if in amazement, whispering to each other. What puzzled me the most was that some of the faces seemed familiar. Misty had given me my sight again in this Other World and what I was able to see was nothing short of unbelievable. Before the fae-touch, I seemed to be moving in slow motion, and within the ring, everything moved so quickly I could only see streaks of white, lavender, green, yellow, and blue lights. There were focal points like the rowan tree and the toadstools that encircled them. When looking around outside the ring I had stepped into everything around it seemed to move in slow motion. It was extraordinary.

I felt very comfortable here. Misty simply smiled and looked so proud of herself in the moment. This was the Other World, a domain hidden from mortal eyes. The world in my dreams and the world that my handsome stranger seemed to elude me in. There was strong magic here, and I could feel it's presence; it filled me with every breath that I took! It seemed to grow inside me, like flowers in a garden blessed with a rich dark soil and showered with warm afternoon sun. Suddenly there was a deep connection to everything—the beings that dwelled there, the earth beneath my feet, everything that was living, plant and animal, and the air that surrounded the very essence of who I was. I seemed to mean something here. I had such a euphoric feeling inside and it was like a drug. As I sat there and looked around me, I knew that I truly belonged. Life smelled sweet and tasted of honey. The warm moonlight softly kissed my skin, and the music soothed my soul. Leaving this place was not an option, I thought as I allowed myself to fall deeper into the moment. Then as quickly as I seemed to have disappeared, I was in a thick fog. The music and chatter quickly faded, and all had ceased. Everything seemed slower now and somehow warped.

A small voice addressed me through the fog, "Titania . . ." It was Misty. "I hoped you would remember once I'd brought you here. I had to bring you to this place during a full moon so that you would be able to return to your world. Most humans who enter the ring of fae are not able to return to the world they once knew. It is forbidden! Do you recognize this place?" Misty asked.

Still dazed, I thought for a moment, as if recalling an old memory.

"This place is quite familiar to me, like home! Everyone looks and seems like family. Is this my home, because if it is, I do not want to return to the human world!" I said adamantly.

"Oh, but you already have returned, dear one. You need to complete yourself in the human world in order to return home for good." Misty replied.

I blinked and found myself lying down within that same circle of toadstools in the night forest, warm and sleepy.

"Was this a dream?" I wondered, but then I happened to look down at my hands. I noticed a beautiful tattoo like decoration on the outside of my left hand. This tattoo was a brilliant sparkling green, dainty swirling lines, as if they were vines growing from my left shoulder, winding down around to my elbow, falling and twisting around my wrist and up the back of my hand. It seemed to come from within my skin; I could feel it moving and alive.

"How could this be? Perhaps it will fade, or maybe someone is trying to play a trick on me." I had to tell myself this because it was totally unbelievable, yet I knew in my heart where I had been and what I had seen. I felt like a queen there, if only in my mindful memories for now.

CHAPTER 4

Secrets

Time seemed to stand still. None seemed to have passed, though I had been there in their presence for what seemed like an immeasurable amount of time. I was lost; it's a terrible thing to feel lost within your own mind. Yet still the mark on my hand remained to remind me of this alternate reality. I had an experience that not many people can say they have had, and I dared not speak of it—not even to my own family.

As I returned home, my husband waited up for me. "Where have you been? I was worried. It seemed like you were gone a long time, are you okay? What's going on?"

How could I answer this question being presented to me at this very moment? I wanted so badly to tell him the truth, because really, no matter what, we were always best friends first! My husband, John, was a gentle man, but could be very stubborn and closed minded sometimes. He always meant well but never seemed to quite get his point across eloquently or with much finesse. He was handsome and kind, and loved me. John was so incredibly human though, and he was always okay with that. He always seemed so satisfied with just being John. This had always fascinated me. It's the reason why I fell in love with him, because no matter what this life brought him, he wouldn't complain or lose his cool.

Fascinating indeed! I could absolutely not relate to this! I had always felt as if I had been plucked out of a different world and placed here in this human world like a chest piece, totally unarmed and alone. This is why John appealed to me so. John was strong like a rock, but sometimes—most of the time—that rock would become unstable. I always felt as if I had to be the one to steady the ground beneath us. This was hardest thing for me to deal with. It was because of his last marriage and the circumstances. I knew that, and I accepted that this was just our situation in life and not fight it. Although everything inside of me wanted to lash out and win the silent war that seemed to be going on in our lives.

I had to quickly give him an answer. "I went for a walk and decided to sit for a while. I must have dosed off, and I wasn't gone that long, was I?" I asked John.

Then I remembered the mark on my left arm and hand! Quickly I took my sleeve and covered it up. Luckily, John didn't notice anything yet.

"No, you weren't gone too long. You were just gone, and it seemed like more time than usual. I know how you like your walks in the moonlight, but I was worried." John said.

"I'm pretty tired. I told you I must have just dozed off for a short time" I replied.

John acted more like a father than a husband. The questioning was unbearable at times for me, and I was not in the mood to answer the barrage of questioning that he was feverously trying to spit out to me all at once. At times it was very difficult for me to absorb and still be gracious.

"Anything new?" I asked.

This was always a loaded question for me to ask because my son Gabriel and husband John were not getting along lately. As Gabriel grew older, his tolerance of the family's situation lessened each day. He grew tired of seeing his mother unhappy. John had a very difficult time dealing with this. This often put me in the middle of a tough situation. I loved my son fiercely and promised myself that he would be raised in a specific way and in a good home. Sometimes John just wasn't with the program I had in my mind. It was quite difficult for John since he wasn't Gabriel's biological father. He just couldn't get past the bloodline issues he had made so important in mind. Gabriel, being the loving soul that he was, was determined to change John's mind.

Gabriel and I had a special bond. I had always felt Gabriel near me even during my childhood. He spoke to my heart, and my soul knew him and of his arrival in my life, perhaps because I willed him into this existence along with me. Gabriel was so very special and dear to me. He was named after the archangel Gabriel for his strength and courage. I knew that Gabriel was an important addition to this human world, and I had made a personal vow that he would be raised knowing that there was something bigger than him, helping him and guiding him through this life, through the very universe. He would be raised with all the knowledge I had and more. I promised that Gabriel would be a decent and great man, and I meant this with all my heart.

I was haunted by my soul memories for as long as I could remember. I often would become lost in my own thoughts of countless memories that I could just barely recollect. My memories were clouded and difficult for me to understand, as if they were in code. Sometimes they seemed like the memories of another person or scenes from a movie. It was hard to put them all together or to even get a moment to myself to calm my thoughts. I was still growing and learning about my new fae-world, still trying to make sense of it all as my life went on as it regularly did, busy and mundane without meaning, just existing to work and watch my money, happiness, hard work, and life go to an ungrateful family (John's ex wife). The only thing that seemed to make sense to me was my son. He was always the one thing that I was able to keep my eyes focused on as the world spun furiously around me uncontrollably. John did not help calm my world. In fact, he had made it more confusing in some ways. John's baggage brought too many unpleasant things into my small world. John was, unfortunately for him, a vessel or conduit for something much darker and sinister that followed him

He had no idea, just that he was among the masses of individuals that had been married, had children, and divorced. He essentially was a pawn in the most evil game of chess for his ex-wife. Her name was truly defining of what she was, Jude. She was truly the "Judas" in his life. I felt this ancient evil and tried to veer my life away from it but got caught up in my human love affair with romance and thought of growing old with someone that I thought I loved enough to overlook this ancient evil being forced upon me. I had false hopes and dreams of actually being with a man who was kind and who loved me, who wanted to have children with me and share in the magical experience of carrying a baby and giving birth. John was the perfect man, he was always patient and sweet with me, and he was the father figure I had longed for in my life. The only problem was that John, at one point in his life, belonged to Jude. Jude and John knew each other through their childhood; therefore, Jude had her footprint on his life, a very magical and strong force of her hand indeed. John, however, was oblivious to this. As far as he knew at the time, this was a "normal" relationship.

They met in a church. They finished high school and then college, got married, and waited to share each other on their wedding night. Next came the children, two to be exact. Problems began with the first pregnancy. Actually, problems began on their wedding night, but John thought it was wedding night jitters and allowed her space to deal with the issues. This was the beginning of a long, hard road of manipulation and ultimate control. Jude had a plan. Still deep within John, he was unsettled and knew that there was something strange happening with the relationship, particularly regarding Jude. Surely, Jude came into this world from a darker realm, I thought. Something—no, everything—within my entire being told me this. There were no prophetic dreams, no ancient wisdom from other worlds to show me what I knew to be so very true regarding Jude, just a cold gut feeling. As the time wore on with John and I, I was able to slowly piece together the puzzle of John and Jude's life together. In fact, it became an unhealthy obsession for me. Slowly it began to become eerily apparent to me that Jude was a little too different, with all the horrible goings-on in John's and my life, and the constant fighting, bad luck, and what I believed to be bad karma.

What exactly was Jude?

CHAPTER 5

Regret

I found myself becoming physically ill and very tired. I thought it had to do with age or working too much; therefore, the stress of my life had to be getting to me. I tried the art of meditation, and one day, while in a meditative state, I had a strange vision. The subject of Jude was not able to leave my mind! It plagued me every day now for ten years. Every waking moment was spent contemplating the evil presence that surrounded me and my pieced-together family. My heart was always sad, as if the joy was slowly being taken from me, and it was. I was actually helping this perpetual evil being set upon me by Jude and did not even realize it. When John and Jude split, Jude vowed that she would make his life miserable and that this was a promise she intended to keep! John said that he thought she meant it, and I could personally testify to this because not only was John truly miserable, I had also been living in a virtual hell with him!

It had been quite puzzling how Jude seemed to have cast a spell on everyone she had come in contact with through the years, especially John's family. John's two sisters thought she was the ultimate human being that could do nothing wrong. Their thoughts of me, however, were quite the contrary. Even though I had rescued their brother from what seemed to be an evil force that had done nothing but put him down his entire life, this did not matter at all to John's family or friends.

Jude had masterfully laid a rocky road ahead for me in particular. From the beginning, Jude wanted the perfect life, and she chose John to be the one to help her create this. They were happy at one time in their lives together. They actually got on with each other very nicely until college. John was not able to finish college because he was obligated to begin the preparation of their lives together. She insisted that she be the one to finish college even though she was a year younger than John, and so began the real manipulation of John's whole world. Jude was busy shaping her own life without concern of John's. Jude had used his love for her and persuasive gifts against him, and it worked every time. Jude was always accustomed to getting what she wanted in her life, and when she didn't, there was guilt-ridden torture to be had by the denying individual.

Jude was not an attractive woman, really, not as you would think her to be. She was, however, manipulative and powerful in her own right. She was short in stature and had very dark-brown eyes with short mousy-brown hair that lay on the top of her head like straw. She never wore makeup or was ever really able to have any sort of style to her at all. Her body was stout and pear shaped, nothing in comparison to me. I was very different, petite as well and my hair was long and dark brown with golden highlights that glimmer in the sun. My eyes were the same color as my hair but with splashes of honey gold, framed by long dark eyelashes. I had an athletic build and seemed to float when I moved. My beauty seemed to emanate from within me, and my smile was what seemed to captivate anyone who encountered me. These attributes that I had were the crowning jewel that fueled the green fires of jealousy inside Jude. Not that I was conceited or think myself fairer than most, but I was certainly not ugly to look at. For no matter what Jude did to herself to try to look better, it paled always to her captivating nemesis. I'm sure Jude would lay awake at night, chanting and muttering how unfair it was that John left her for me. Jude would have many nights when "friends" would come over to visit while she chanted and chatted the same mantra of how unfair and horrible John and I were, and I am certain that her loyal friends chimed in as they should to help her feel better about her situation.

Jude was casting spells each day with those strong feelings and hatred she carried, and instilling the help from unaware people she liked to refer to as "her people." These spells and wishes were fueled by fury and jealousy and false pride, all sent out to the universe and being answered with great obedience as if she had her own genie in her pocket.

How dare they move on with their lives when she wasn't ready for her life to change? The odd part of Jude's story is that she asked John to leave three times. Unbeknownst to her, on the third time that John was asked to leave, he did!

What magic was this? Jude was a quiet mystic with evil undertones! She knew what she was and had a focused purpose in her life on this earth plane: to harm me in every way she could, even inadvertently kill me if need be!

During one of my meditations I had a vision of Jude and Misty. There were no words, but Misty seemed to be very worried and nervous around Jude. It was a vision that I was having about the Other World, and I felt as though Misty was trying to tell me something. At first it was hard to piece together. Jude was the last person I wanted to encounter during a meditation, but Misty was showing me what seemed to be yet another place that was connected to the Other World. This world was not as inviting, nor was it lighthearted and beautiful. Then I began to realize what I was seeing. There was a dark place just outside the Other World. There were sentries or guards placed on the outskirts of the Other World to ensure nothing crossed over. I found my self recalling something I had been warned of long ago, but had forgotten about. I tried to locate old legends and books on whatever I could find on my vision, and surprisingly found a plethora of information. I was able to locate certain lineages and stories regarding the old wars between the faeries.

Jude came from an underground realm of what is called the dark folk of the fae. Jude never knew of the true realm of faerie before the coming of the dark realm she knew so well, for she was born of this dark place, thanks to her full dark fae mother. Her father, however, was an unaware kindly human. These dark fae beings were once considered part of the faerie realm until one of them decided to challenge the royal fae (and this was never to be done)! These were the folk that kept not only the balance and peace in the fae realm but also the peace and calm between the worlds of fae and humans. Jude was a direct descendant of the one who provoked the challenge.

They were fierce and fought in typical fae form, dirty and cruel! Dark and forbidden magic was used without a second thought. Once the fae committed to this dark magic, they were automatically banished from the beautiful warmth of the sun in the heavenly fae realm. This did not bother the group that challenged the royals. Nicoli was the dark provoker's name. He was in love with one of the royals, my mother, Corina, who died while giving birth to me. Nicoli knew he could never have Corina, and each day the jealousy burned inside him until he could contain himself no more. He was quite a persuasive court royal and very convincing to the people that doubted the royals.

Nicoli had the gift that was passed on in his family: the power of intoxicating groups of people, making them believe that he was powerful and intelligent with good intentions. Though Nicoli's family had this gift with groups of people, they did not have this power over just one individual at a time, usually. Therefore, Nicoli had the idea of turning to the ancient scrolls regarding the dark faerie magic that was always considered forbidden.

Why did it even exist? you ask. Well, why does good and evil exist? Because it must, as it is part of the balance of our universe. Regardless of the consequences. Jude was of the same clan as Nicoli (her uncle), although she was far more selfish and evil than he was even though she was only half fae, her evil intentions made up for the half human blood that she had. Her focus was on one thing: obtaining the perfect human life. She had no idea that she was part fae. All she knew was that whatever she thought of with great intensity came to fruition, albeit through her dreams or some sort of guide to help lead her to her endeavors—life and all the money she could need and the adoration of everyone who ever knew her. Jude became lost in her human ways; she was utterly infatuated with being human and with herself as a human!

Her uncle Nicoli was always able to speak to a group and have them absolutely captivated. They would be willing to give up everything that was dear to them; even their own children were left behind to fight a battle that would doom them all to a dark place of existence forever without the joy that came with the light that is the universe. This was truly dark, unblessed faerie magic at work, and there were many followers, to the royal's surprise. The fae folk that chose this path fought as if under a spell and without feelings for the others they once loved! The battle was on a dark moon in late autumn, and it came without warning. This is how Nicoli liked it most! Darkness, availing and encapsulating the unaware. Pure essence of evil awaiting the taste of blood in which he craved most, the blood of the royals and all who followed, especially my father, the king of all the fae.

CHAPTER 6

The Dark Battle

Nicoli had been contemplating this attempt of war for many years. He was not stupid. He took himself to the Great Hall on several different occasions to study diligently the art of warfare and the use of dark magic. He learned of forbidden spells and the summoning of demons that would aid in his selfish cause. None questioned him as he was a highly regarded member of the fae court in an earlier time. He chose to be in this position in order to be close to his queen, Corina. He tried, on several occasions, to seduce her, befriend her, and gain her trust, especially when her king was away.

King Elwyn always had too much to tend to. It was not just the business of the fae world, but the reintegration of the humans into the fae world as well. This movement/prophecy was thought to be an impossible myth by most and disregarded as loose talk and not reality, but the earthly realm was dying and becoming more of a hellish place than the Great Creator first intended it to be. The fae were the custodial guardians of the land, caring tenderly for the two dimensions and all that lived in them. The faeries once had free rein and were quite close to the human race and were highly regarded as the guardians of Mother Nature herself. This slowly disappeared throughout the millennia, and soon the faeries were forced to move on to a higher realm or frequency of living due to the mistreatment and disbelief from the very humans they were watching over. The faeries have always been closer to the Great Creator, and only the royals—the faeries that were most grounded, the faeries that shared the human DNA strand—were made privy to this secret prophecy by Nila, the being that is the voice for the Great Creator.

King Elwyn had always felt the need to help the prophecy and have a good outcome for all beings of this world, no matter what origin, animal or otherwise. Not all the faerie folk knew of the prophecy in great detail, and it was best that way. Over many years of existence after the official banishment from the earth realm, the faerie folk evolved and broke into different societies and clans. They interbred and broke off into different belief systems. Some fled to the sea, some to the hills of Ireland, worshiping the gold and treasure that they liked to keep near to them. They really were no different than the humans in most respects. In certain writings it is written that Nila revealed once very long ago that the Great Creator was contemplating ceasing the existence of all living creatures forever without the promise of a new. This burden was for King Elwyn to bear regardless of the cost to him personally. He promised Nila that he would make things right, since the Great Creator found the grace to make him king of both these realms. There had been several different human kings and rulers of the earth realm, and all failed miserably to do the task.

King Elwyn had always been kind and modest. He was levelheaded and cared more for every other living creature than anything or anyone the Great Creator had ever seen. He was the Solomon of both realms. Best of all, King Elwyn was a delightful surprise, and Nila had been monitoring this since his creation. Nila was the lady of the waters, the keeper of all secrets great and holy. The most trusted being of the Great Creator, Nila was the keeper of the universal conduit and most precious substance of all: water. In face her name means blue water.

Nila was a faerie household name, but she never appeared randomly to just anyone. No, Nila was the voice of the one and was only meant to be heard by the most cherished faerie to the Great Creator. This made things difficult even for King Elwyn and his wife. They both were quite familiar with Nila, but no one else ever was. Even with the matured faerie community, with all their set beliefs, they still had some doubts and reservations because they had not seen Nila for themselves. She was legend and nothing more to them.

Tensions soon began to rise in the faerie realm, and its people were becoming uneasy. Doubts began to arise around King Elwyn and the other royals. Eventually the prophecy was spoken about as if it were only a child's story. There were many faeries who did not like the humans and would much rather see a world without them in it. The humans were thought of as vile, empty creatures for the most part. It was hard to believe they even had a soul. They were quickly destroying the land we all shared and neglected it. This is how most faeries saw humans and drew from in their lifetimes, and the hatred grew as rapidly as the human destruction of Mother Nature. Even though the humans had been unaware of their faerie brethren, they simply had no idea that they were destroying an entire race of beings that shared their lands. The humans did not realize, nor did they seem to care that in the careless treatment of the earth and sea, they were making the faerie world smaller and harder to keep alive. Every, plant, tree, and animal cried out in pain from the earth realm. The cries fell upon deaf human ears, however the faeries heard every whimper. The humans were never taught to believe in anything but themselves, and it was truly astonishing that the stories about their god survived for as long as it had even when the stories of the human book had been twisted and misinterpreted. Only King Elwyn carried the true book with him at all times, and he was strictly instructed by Nila not to share this with anyone. He would know when the right time would be, and that time had not come just yet.

The evil and jealous Nicoli took advantage of his position in the fae court and held secret meetings, first with two then six, then the groups grew larger until he was ready to strike. This is the brief history of Jude's family tree. This tree was as twisted and dark as an old knotted vine, and so was she. "No mercy" was the motto of Jude's creed. To everyone else, Jude appeared to be a wonderful and caring human being, as with her uncle Nicoli. She was the perfect wife, mother, friend, employee, and sister-in-law, and she was a model citizen. Yet underneath her human facade lurked a dark and bitter being with an agenda full of rage and revenge for John and now me and my son.

Meanwhile, I still had a life to live, and sometimes life would demand certain lessons from me. Life itself showed no mercy—no rest for the weary. It would go on despite what others might do to the good or bad people of this world. I felt torn. I often found myself daydreaming about my life while at work and often wondered why I wasn't as blessed as the people in Michael's life or anyone else's for that matter. It really was a shame because Michael and I seemed to be perfect for each other. Day after day, this was proven to me time and again. I wondered if maybe I was a greater part of Michael's life but living instead in an alternate dimension, a synchronicity of lifetimes as his true partner, the one I felt that I was meant to be with. Each time Michael spoke of his life, I would feel so proud inside as if I were the life he was speaking of, but not so, not yet.

So why the strong feelings of belonging to someone else and not to my beloved John? I loved John very much. He was like an old friend to me, comfortable and warm, but there was too much familiarity with Michael, and it actually frightened me. As time passed, the daydreaming became worse, and my dreams of Michael became more vivid. I had thoughts of how my life should be, and each time I heard Michael spew the lovely recollections he had of his wife, Ciara, I was more convinced that I had been cheated in this human experience somehow that is my life.

I wondered how life could be so unfair, and I was feeling like a spoiled child. I always felt that I deserved so much more than what I had. I blamed myself for so much; was I greedy, selfish, deceitful, and too regal for my poor life? I felt I should be more sheltered and taken care of than I had been, not just loved and left to fend for the necessities that my son Gabriel and I required. These unfortunate thoughts were commonplace in my mind because of my situational circumstances with John and Jude. Jude had succeeded in helping create a place of fire and brimstone, a purgatory of karmic payback for me. It truly was a sad situation because John and I had the ability to be happy, had we ever been given the chance. I wondered if this was truly my destiny to continue to live in the persecution created for the sins I had never committed. Have I created this reality for myself, and if so, how could I change it for the better?

CHAPTER 7

Irish Trickery

Michael's wife, Ciara, was usually in the background, running the show in their lives. He always spoke well of her though and never shared or alluded to any problems or difficulties. Although he spoke too well of their life together, it was disconcerting really, and it always raised a red flag in my mind. There were countless hours of having to hear the stories of where they would travel and how wonderful of a time they had and what trip would be next. He was always speaking of the wonderful weekends and expensive dinners out. There was date night and "time alone" and anything else that could be the most sickening thing one could think of that would always complete the perfect picture of happiness in a seemingly perfect world of Michael and Ciara.

For a while I was able to endure these stories, but once everyone else decided to be involved in Michael's life and to participate, it all became too much to take. I'm sure Michael had no idea how truly painful it was for me to hear the details of his perfect lifestyle, but when he spoke of Ciara wanting a daughter, that was the knife driven through the very heart of me. I wanted very dearly to have a daughter of my own; this was something else that Jude had systematically taken from me as well. My husband John was told that he should get himself taken care of and had vasectomy right before Jude and he divorced. I believe John thought it would appease Jude somehow, maybe it was a last ditch effort to keep the marriage? Of course John had no idea he would meet somebody younger that might want to have a baby with him? In other words John had absolutely no idea I was coming. I suppose he wouldn't, he was only human, and very short sighted.

Still there was something between Michael and I that could not be denied. At first I thought of it as a basic attraction, but as time went on, there were certain subtleties. I would often catch him staring at me, then once our eyes would seem to meet, he would abruptly turn away, pretending to have never been looking at me at all. When I would be working, Michael would be sure to be around me somehow, fumbling and fiddling with whatever it was he could find. I thought that perhaps I was imagining things, until one day.

As I performed my normal duties, I noticed Michael watching me again. I pretended not to notice, but it did make me smile. After all it was flattering. It was as if I could feel his thoughts.

"So how are you doing?" asked Michael, making the question seem business-related.

"What?" I asked.

"I asked you how you were. Did you not hear me, or are you choosing to ignore me again?" asked Michael as he stood closer to me to help me with some of my day's work.

I was a little shocked and confused because no one really helped me at all with this part of my job, so this was quite nice. Very nice indeed, since Michael was the one standing so very close to me that I could feel the heat radiating from him softly.

As we worked, he joked with me and moved closer, our sides softly touching. It was a familiar yet comfortable feeling, something remembered from a dream long ago. There was something. I couldn't put my finger on it, but I was sure he felt it too.

Oftentimes in the mornings, though I wasn't sure exactly whom it was that I might be working with, I would just know it was Michael. My senses were so tuned into his that as I walked through the first door, I could smell his cologne. I would tell myself, "It's Michael, I know it!" There he sat in his normal spot, awaiting my arrival.

"Good morning, killer, how are you?" he said as he smiled—that brilliant heart-melting smile that seemed to get me every time. Even when I was at my lowest, all Michael had to do was say my name and simply smile. It wasn't fair, how perfect he seemed to me. No human should be this perfect—his hair, his smell, the brilliant smile that captivated my attention. I walked in, looking straight at him with a quick "Good morning," and rushed passed. It was all too much to take in at once.

There were times that I was unable to control my body as it physically ached for him somehow. It was unbearable at times to be in the same room with him. I longed to set myself free and dared to imagine what would happen if I did. Would time dare to stand still for that moment, and when would the right moment be? Most importantly, would he be open to me and return the same feelings? This is what I was the most unsure of! What was possessing me to have these thoughts and feelings? It felt not of this earth, as if I were tapping into a separate universe or existence.

Michael was an interesting guy; he didn't seem as though he had the same thoughts. As a matter of fact, as far as I was concerned, he didn't like me at all; I was simply just a coworker that he felt obliged to be kind to. I felt like a pretty little doll up on a shelf that would get some attention from him every once in a while then put back upon that shelf carelessly and left there wondering when I would be admired again by him if at all, but there were concerns running through his mind as well. Once in a while we may have a short conversation that might include some feelings. Words hidden within words, a verbal path impossible to follow. He would share that he wondered about me too, always admiring how well I took care of myself and how lovely he thought I was. He really couldn't help but notice, and this made him nervous. Sometimes he would comment on my perfume. He seemed to like my favorite and knew the exact name of it. He wanted me to know he admired it but had to keep his guard and distance always while he was around me. He was afraid that once he let his guard down, his life, and mine as we knew it would change dramatically, and he would not be able to restrain himself despite of the personal vows he had taken with Ciara. He also had my best interest in mind and couldn't bear the thought of causing heartache or pain in my life.

Michael thought, *what is wrong with me? I am a professional. I could lose everything, Titania could loose even more!* As Titania walked by, I would take her into my gaze and have thoughts of grabbing her and holding her close to me. I just wanted so badly to stare deeply into those eyes and kiss the soft pink lips I long to taste. I wanted to taste her, smell her, touch her but found myself bound by something greater than my need to be with her. I knew that it wouldn't take much to get there, and I felt her tremble each time I happened to brush by her. Sometimes I would experiment with myself and stand as close to Titania as I possibly could without touching her. The space between us became electric and the air was supercharged. I would stay as long as I permitted myself without being too obvious to the others we worked with, or for as long as I could physically stand it. There was an energy that had been missing from my life with Ciara. The fire of life existed with the most unsuspecting person known to me, Titania, a simple little lab technician that happened to work with me every so often. I was just able to take advantage of the little times we had together

CHAPTER 8

Curiosity

There seemed to be such intimacy between us, and I could see Michael fight his feelings every so often. Michael could be so charming and funny and seemed like he enjoyed my company. Tragically though, there were the times that Michael would become almost cruel and indifferent toward me, hurting my feelings and belittling me to the benefit of the others that we worked with. This confused me tremendously and really hurt. I was not an ugly, stupid, or cruel person at all; I was caring and forthright, with my heart on my sleeve and the pains of my life tattooed on my soul like the weight of the ages. Yes, we were both involved in our own relationships in this life, but Michael's soul was calling out my name, and this was hard to ignore. I often thought of my life as if I were trapped behind a glass window, looking out and able to see what it was I needed, wanted, and deserved, only to find that I could only press myself up against the glass to view and admire, but nothing else. Michael was neither friend nor foe and was not willing to establish anything certain or tangible with me. Perhaps his fears became too much for him as well, or maybe he was just selfish and wanted to stay in his little comfort zone?

I looked forward to my time at work. This seemed like the only place that Jude was not able to reach me. My life was better at work, almost the way it should be and with whom I felt connected to, but it was only work. Once in a while, events would be planned, and when they were, Michael seemed excited but anxious about them. If I asked for anything of him, he was unable to refuse me (within reason). Michael was always willing to go the extra mile for me and keep it quiet so that no one else would be able to make their own assumptions or start any vicious rumors. We both fit together like a puzzle—so why the extra pieces?

Damn faeries, never can wait for anything, no patience whatsoever! If I am a faerie that would explain a lot! I thought.

I knew I was somehow connected to the faerie realm and that I had no patience at all, but was Michael connected too?

Through the years, I was able to learn so much of the faerie folk—where they hid, who they were, how they were. I learned of some of their speech and that some were appointed human guardians. Some faeries were warriors, troublemakers, and wish grantors. Oh, not like the type you know in children's movies; they were tricky and cruel, not nice beautiful women or grandmothers just waiting to take care of you. No! They would steal your life spirit and lock it away like a jewel until the elvyn became aware and gave you back to the Great Creator. This was bad faerie magic, and the elves were a type of law keepers of the realm. I learned that souls are very complicated energy sources. Sought out for the magic each one carries. If a faerie could have a human soul, they could summon anything they desire. Sometimes it was everlasting youth, or turn it into a weapon of great power. The energy a soul carries is the equivalent of several atomic bombs, and if that energy is harnessed, just imagine what it could be used for?

These stories were told to me when I was young by my grandmother and mother. Although, my mother was much more guarded when speaking of faerie world more so than my grandmother ever was. My mother would avoid speaking of them. I could tell she was frightened and tried not to have a second thought of them, but later some of these stories were confirmed by close friends familiar with this realm. I would imagine which group of faerie I might belong to. I had my ideas about it based on my brief contact with Misty and what she seemed to look like. Although Misty reminded me of the folk that interbred with butterflies and insects, she seemed to have some elf in her as well. This made this particular species quite breathtaking. Most faeries were able to take on a human form and quite often liked to live as humans, but they had the ability to fade away and return to the Other World. I, however, seemed to not have this option so my fantasy lineage remained a mystery. Misty would visit me, but it would always be when I was mostly dreaming. It was a rare occasion for us to interact the way we did in the faerie ring.

Misty was bound by certain rules and laws; therefore, she could not visit me outside of the dream realm as often as I would have liked. During these dream visitations I would learn more about the faeries and other dimensions. Until one day I was not feeling myself, and I sat on a bench just outside my home in the forest. It was a late afternoon, dusk, my favorite most relaxing time of the day, and I began to daydream. I drifted quickly as the warm, soft rays of the autumn sun gently kissed my skin through the leaves of the trees that swayed softly in the breeze. Then came a low humming noise; it grew and grew until I was forced to take notice. It wasn't a bee; it was Misty! A visit from Misty was always a pleasant surprise because this was proof to me that I wasn't losing my mind or imagining things, but usually a visit meant that there was something serious about to be revealed to me.

Misty was always so sweet and made me feel as if I had a cute little guardian angel on the other side.

"How be you today, lady?" Misty whispered.

I was happy to see Misty but so very sad in my heart about my life. It was something I couldn't' get past, and I felt myself falling into depression. I did not look forward to the conversation we were about to have.

Misty felt this and asked, "Why aren't you happy to see me, lady?"

"I'm happy, Misty, I am! I tell you I have missed you, but my life is just a mess, Misty," I explained as I began to cry a little. "You are truly a blessed sight for these sore eyes. Each time you appear to me, I realize that I am not crazy." I said.

"Oh, Lady Titania, you are anything but! I miss you too! You know that I have come to you to warn you of certain events and things to come. I take such a risk with Nila when I do this," Misty whispered.

"Nila? Who is this? I have heard this name before as if in a dream or in passing," I asked.

"Nila is the one, the only that helps guide us all. She is what we are here to protect. She is what the Great Creator has made to be his own. She is the voice of him, his thought. She is the four winds and the moon. Nila is life itself, the mother of nature, Titania. You must tell me what it is that troubles you so, my dear friend." Misty asked.

As this question was posed to me, I thought for a moment and tried to gather myself. After all, what wasn't wrong? I had too much going on, so much to face, and now burdened with confusion, and thoughts of self doubt that was creeping in like a storm brewing. It was all too much. I was stuck, stuck in this world with seemingly nowhere to go and without a purpose. Nothing seemed to make me happy except the distant thoughts that I had of Michael, or possibly leaving this world completely.

"I feel tormented, Misty. I no longer want to speak to my friends, and I can barely function as a wife and mother. I am a depressed and angry individual. I can no longer recognize who I am. I ask myself every day if I could ever feel joy again, but I fear that I will not if I stay here in this life. It is not really John I have the problem with, but I know in my heart that Jude will never go away. I almost fear that she will follow me no matter where I go. I could run away but fear it would be too late because she has already cursed me, and there is a complication. I am constantly confused by this person I've met, his name is Michael. At times I feel he is interested in me and wants to be closer, but I know this could never be because we are both married. Misty, I can't stop thinking of him. He is always on my mind, in my dreams, and I carry him with me everywhere I go. I'd rather not have these thoughts and I would like them to go away! This is making things worse for me, and I hate myself for it. I hate this world and the rules that it has! I can't think straight and just want to sit alone most of the time," I answered Misty with quite a mouthful.

"I know of your plight. That is why I have come. To help you sort things out. Tell me what you feel about Michael," Misty urged.

"Well, he is so familiar to me, and when we are in the same room, I feel, well, I feel . . ." I could not put this into words. It was difficult, for it was not a human feeling at all.

"You feel?" asked Misty.

"The last time Michael and I merely brushed against each other, he held both of my arms and sort of pulled me close to him. When that happened, I felt like I had a rush of electricity run through my whole body. Misty, I almost fell into his arms completely. I actually shook from it. It really frightened me, and I wondered if he could feel it too. Weird, right?" I asked.

"No! Not weird. You must try to remember, you are not of this world, and neither is Michael! What you both consider 'normal' in your human form is quite different when in your true form. For example, the process of lovemaking is not what you would think it to be. When you are of faerie blood, there is a process that must occur. Remember, we are on a much higher frequency than the humans and are a much older breed. The Great Creator has blessed us with a fiery blood coupled with an ornate desire for whatever it is that we want. Our senses are heightened, and we must partake in each other's energy source when both individual faeries are prepared to share themselves. They must be in their faerie form in order to perform this love ritual and will find themselves transforming, unable to continue the glamour they had placed on themselves to appear human. All the facades the glamour puts up and the control we had as a human is no more. Anything that would be considered rules or law does not matter. The only thing that matters is acquiring the energy from the other and the taste of his or her flesh. Don't look so surprised. It is not as though we devour each other's flesh. We must just taste of it. I have heard that when twin souls have the opportunity to partake in this ritual, it can be quite an incredible experience!. I myself have not had this opportunity, but you and Michael, now this would be something. I am here to tell you that Michael is your betrothed from our world.

He is not a prince but comes from royal faerie bloodlines. Your father and mother chose him for you many, many years ago before you were born. You both knew each other in the faerie realm. That is why he seems so familiar to you. Both of your souls have been split in twine. One follows the other always until the time is right. This has to do with the prophecy that has been passed down to us all through the ages. This would explain your many dreams of the individual whose face has been hidden from you until now. He must visit you and be near you in the dream state and you to his. Nila said that your journey in particular would not be an easy one, since you are of the prophecy itself. Your father will not speak of it, nor will Nila, in much detail. We that are closest to you do not know much, just bits and pieces of a story that has been passed down for many years.

"Also, Titania, there is the matter of Jude. You already know that Jude is part of the dark realm of faeries and she is here to stay until you become aware and focused of what you truly are. She is what we call a dark sprite. She is of the fallen faeries, very bitter, very tricky. She would be willing to wait one thousand years to see you both suffer, especially you! The only good thing is that she is unaware that she is part of this dark realm, a half-breed. You must understand that the negative energy Jude produces is the dark magic that binds you! It is what keeps your magic at bay. Whenever you feel stifled, it is the dark power that keeps you blind to your truth. She does not want to see you become anything other than miserable, for fear of her own consequences, as they would be rather severe in her mind in her human existence. Once you realize that you are a much stronger being than her and are able to free yourself of this human condition, you would be able to control this human life you are in with the power of the universe. This power is yours for the taking to use at your will. Jude would then seem powerless to you. She would still be there but not have the chokehold she has on you in particular. For now, you have given her far too much power over you, expecting that John would protect you from her wrath, which he has not!

"As for your human John, this is another story. He should have known better than to allow Jude to get this close to you. You see, human guardians are appointed unbeknownst to them. They are particularly bound by their worldly rules and laws. One of which is to protect that which you love and allow nothing to harm or penetrate the family bond. He was not allowed to marry you as this is a forbidden practice, especially with you being who you are in our realm. You, however, are hard to say no to. This is why you have had so much trouble with all of your relationships and so many failed human marriage bonds. You look too hard for your twin soul, and now that you have found him, he appears to be in the same predicament as you. He is much better off, however, because he has no Jude there to make his life hellish, but this is not his test. It is yours. John should have followed his human laws much more than he has. You have been infiltrated by the dark one, and she is taking full advantage of John's mistakes! She knows him like her favorite book.

"All she needs to do is turn to the proper page, and she has all her answers there right in front of her. Your faerie father is quite disappointed in John and is currently contemplating his doom, but have no fear of this yet. We must discuss your faerie gifts. You are able to see people for what they are for they cannot hide from your sight. So tell me what you thought of Michael's wife Ciara," asked Misty.

"Well, I immediately thought of a leprechaun. Dumb, right?" I asked.

"No, not dumb at all. She is of the leprechaun clan of faeries. She is a type of faerie. People often think of the leprechaun as predominately male, but they need to procreate, don't they? So there are the female versions, and they are even more greedy than the males. They are a class of faerie folk associated in Irish mythology and folklore, as with all faeries, with Tuatha Dé Danann [the goddess Danu], and inhabited Ireland before the arrival of the Celts. Usually they take the form of old men who enjoy partaking in mischief, but in this case, Ciara has fallen for your betrothed and decided to sink her claws deeply into him. They are said to be very rich, having many treasure crocks buried during wartime. This is, unfortunately, what is appealing to Michael right now, and everyone that are his friends help reinforce this desire. He enjoys his comfortable life in this human form, and Ciara knows this. According to legend, if any one human keeps an eye fixed upon a leprechaun, he cannot escape, but the moment the gaze is withdrawn, he vanishes. Favorably for us, Michael is not human, but he does not realize this yet. He is not ready to realize this. He is of the same clan as you and I, of course! This is what makes me infuriated with Ciara. I have always disliked the leprechauns, dirty little buggers. You just can't trust them, not a one. How exactly did she act toward you when you met her?" asked Misty with great anticipation.

"Well, I found her odd," I replied. "She seemed a strong, overbearing personality, and quite frankly, I liked her very little. I just couldn't grasp what it was that Michael saw in her. She was not attractive. She had a low murky energy to her, and her main focus was having a child. I couldn't even see a closeness between them. It seemed as though they were more acquaintances rather than husband and wife. When I tried to engage in conversation with her, she backed away immediately and put her focus on anything else but what I had to say. It seemed as though that Michael was just following her orders and not very interested in her babble.

"I truly found it puzzling that she would not speak to me in normal conversation. Rather, she spoke through Michael, diverting all the attention onto herself. I don't know. I wondered if I was just imagining what was happening and if Michael had noticed the same." I said.

"Know this, Titania, Ciara is not able to physically be near you for long periods of time because of what she is. It is forbidden, but they are tricksters and have powerful magic. Whatever magic she has thrown on Michael is strong, and now that they are speaking of having a child, the magic veil she has cast has grown even stronger. The leprechaun has gone too far. She saw what she wanted and got greedy, knowing that she should not have taken things to this level. She has interfered with the prophecy and will be dealt with when she is caught, be sure of that!" Misty replied.

This was the most Misty had ever said to me all at once, and it was overwhelming! Although, most of what I thought was definitely confirmed. Faeries can be tricky beings, but Misty was of a different sort. Misty was a trusted guardian of the fae realm, seemingly appointed to me by Nila. This rush of information did not help my human situation, however. Still there were bills to be paid and lawyers to hire, bad credit, no money to be had, and all this because of Jude. I felt as if I was in quick sand, and as I looked up all around me, I could see my loved ones—John, my human mother, my grandmother, etc.—but no one helping me out of my pit of despair. The sand was relentless and continued to methodically fall grain by grain into the pit until I would be no more! Misty could see me start to tear up again and decided to take her leave. All at once a flash of light and she was gone, bidding me good-bye in an echoed whisper.

"I shall return to you, lady, soon I shall return. Remember what I say, and please do what it is that you feel, for you are of faerie blood! Remember, I will not be far from you!" Misty's voice echoed through the air.

CHAPTER 9

Change Is Eminent

There was no denying it. I was changing inside. I could feel it, mentally and physically. I returned home and went about my normal routine, made dinner, helped with homework, and entertained my husband. There never seemed to be any time left for just me. Sure, I was able to sit for a while from time to time, but those moments were few and far between. Since I was going through this virtual metamorphosis, I seemed to crave more from life itself. More stimulation was required, and I was extra sensitive to my environments. Home was home, no changes there really; everything remained the same chaotic mess with all the normal duties. Work, however, was quite different. I noticed people noticing me more often. I no longer seemed to fade into the shadowy background.

As Michael arrived, he noticed me right away, although he did not say a word to me, just a simple "Good morning. How were things this morning?" He waited though, waited until we were alone to say that simple good morning.

This had to be because everyone that worked closest to us felt an unusual compulsion to squash whatever it was that they saw between Michael and I, and it all seemed to revolve around Ciara.

Once Michael and I were alone and walking to have lunch, he stopped me.

"You look different today, brighter. Did you do something with your hair?" Michael asked.

"No," I replied.

"Hmm, something is different. Your eyes, are you wearing contacts, working out, something? I can't pinpoint it, but you seem as if you are glowing. Are you . . ." Michael could barely ask the question, "pregnant?"

I giggled. "No, Michael, I've told you it's not possible with John, remember?"

"Oh yeah, yeah, I remember." Michael replied.

It was an uncomfortable silence for a moment, as he simply stared at me out of the corner of his eye. My features were a bit more prominent, my hair was slightly darker, my eyes were a bit more yellow/gold, and I seemed more graceful and sure of myself. For the rest of the day, Michael watched my every move, studying me, noticing that I appeared to move slower as if in a dance. My hair swung about me as if it were floating, and it began to fascinate him even more than he already was.

Michael always seemed to be in control of everything, his life, his family, money, career, etc. He was regimented; he had a routine: Sunday church, morning workouts, specific diet, fine taste in food and wine, trips, friends that loved him, and of course Ciara. It was as if they were both celebrities within their circle of friends. When he was at work, he seemed relaxed, and everyone loved him. I, however, would study him—the way he moved, what he wore, how he spoke, how he smelled, his hair, his smile— but most of all, his mannerisms toward me was what counted most. As for the others in the office, they all seemed on edge and grumpy, and they tried with all their might to destroy what it was that was undeniable. Michael and I were destined to be together centuries ago, and now finally in this life, something was about to happen, regardless of the human restrictions we had! Misty's words rung once again inside of my head, about what faerie love was like. *She spoke as if I were some kind of royalty.* The thought was quickly dismissed from my mind. *How could that be anyway, who am I, and who is he?* These thoughts were all-consuming and slowly beginning to drive me insane.

Michael's moods were ever changing, and as the weeks wore on, he became worse. Sometimes it seemed as if he almost missed me; at other times, it was as if I were invisible and didn't matter at all. This was completely intolerable, and I was losing my patience with everything.

I was no pushover! *I do not need to ask for what I want. It comes to me! How dare he think he is better than me, or even if that leprechaun Ciara is better than me!* I thought to myself, and the more I thought about this, the angrier I became. I could feel my emotions becoming more intense and harder to control. *What am I, an animal or angel or both, and what does it matter anyhow?* These thoughts raced through my mind as I worked through my day, looking around the lab and casually glancing over toward Michael looking over some newly posted pictures on the Internet that his Ciara had recently posted for all to see. *Does he think I'm stupid? I can feel you watching me, you fiend. You are neither friend nor foe to me, so what of you?* The words in my head became more and more angered and were loud as I screamed them inside my head, and the frustration was beginning to show on my face. I became uncomfortably silent and spoke to no one, not even Michael, especially not him!

Soon it was time to leave for the day, and I could not wait to get away and get home. I needed to meditate and focus. Once my thoughts came into focus, this became a potentially dangerous thing. Of course, I performed my normal duties as a mother and a wife (always), but it was good to get some needed time to myself to compose my thoughts and emotions. Usually when I felt these intense changes, they were typically accompanied by a visit from the faeries.

It was getting colder now, and autumn was well in place. This was my favorite time of the year. This always seemed to be a happy time for me, no matter what the circumstances. It was quite pleasurable to be outside on an autumn day at dusk. As I settled in for the afternoon, I stepped into the garden outside, fully surrounded by the forest that engulfed my home. I looked all about and sniffed the air. It would rain that evening, and I could feel the electricity in the air. There would be thunderstorms too. However my thoughts lingered on Michael, constantly wondering about the future and what was being shared with me by my new faerie friends.

I felt absolutely idiotic and hateful of myself for the thoughts and feelings that I was experiencing.

Why couldn't he have stayed a dream, or was it me that needed him to become real, so I made him up? If I were to unleash my true desires of what it is that I want, he would be helpless. Would it be just another mistake that I would be potentially saddled with for twenty-two more years in this pathetic life I am stuck in? Or is this my true destiny? Misty did say that he is my betrothed, but does he know that? I am doubtful of his connection to me, and I can't help but be so completely irritated by that individual he claims to be his wife. Her insignificant face haunts me. Does she do it on purpose, or is she just unwittingly and inexcusably that much of an annoyance!

So many thoughts in my head, and none made sense. All I knew was what I had seen and what I had been told. Ridiculously a fantastical and unbelievable truth? Who in god's name would ever believe me now?

CHAPTER 10

Thoughts and Decisions

Thoughts raced through my head, always wondering about every moment and decision I had ever made. Every thought I had now was questioned by my inner voice. Although, I felt like I was completely insane. The dynamics of every situation in my life held entirely too much confusion, and no one can live with that much doubt and that much guilt. There was so much more I should be thinking about, especially the problems that John and Jude brought to the table—John with his poor planning and financial faux pas, and the greed of life and elicit self-appointed aristocratic behavior that Jude displayed with her presence on this earth by the second.

It is unfortunately not up to me to make such judgments on people, but I can always wonder why such behavior is continually allowed. If I am what I think I am, why couldn't I pass judgment on Jude and Ciara? Perhaps it is not for me to pass the judgment on Ciara, because I am simply not sure of Michael as of yet. How truly confused is he, and is he a frickin part of some grander plan as I am? He certainly isn't acting like "my betrothed", however I can feel myself changing, and when I am around him, I feel the change occur rapidly. It's as though I am about to lose control of something wild inside myself. I wonder if people are beginning to notice the changes I am feeling? My husband seems fine at times, and at times, I feel that I wouldn't mind spending the rest of my life with him, but it is a most ominous thought to know that Jude would always be there, leering at us through the darkness, hoping for the worst, and John letting her have it so unwittingly. Could I bear that for the rest of my life? Furthermore, could Gabriel? How fair is it to him? It stands to reason there is more to this faerie story than I am being told about.

Regardless of all else, there was my son Gabriel, sweet boy that he was, ever so vigilant toward me, his mother, and always willing to help me when he could. It was somewhat easier now that he was a teenager, but the mood swings were horrible, especially when it came to him and John. It was always a match between them. I could never figure out if they loved each other or simply just tolerated their company. This was truly a test of patience for me. This was a difficult time this human life presented to me, but why me?

What was it about certain people in this life? I didn't know Ciara and really didn't want to, but she seemed to be in the right place at the right time, didn't she? No horrible ex-wife for her. No! She would just become the same type of ex-wife in the human form and make Michael miserable. I was sure of it! Surely he must see this.

Yet here was my poor son, trying to survive along with me, always hoping for the best for our family, mostly for me. This is what truly made my blood boil over with Jude. No one questioned her actions at all. It was just assumed that the other person that had "done her wrong" was wrong, and that was that! How in the Great Creator's name could this be? Still I sat back and watched my son suffer as an indirect result of her actions toward John. We lived our lives unsure of the next day, and here was Michael and Ciara showing off. Ciara was always pushing and shoving their lives in front of everyone else every chance she got. The internet is not my friend right now! Perhaps I wouldn't be as bitter about her as I was now because of what I had learned about Michael from Misty. I subconsciously had taken hold of this idea and made it real, and now I was mad about it all—mad that this horrible little leprechaun had tried to steal what was rightfully mine—and I despised her for it! My feelings were strong now, much stronger than they had ever been. This came with the rushing faerie blood within me.

I had to begin to learn how to calm myself, and as I spoke aloud, I seemed to quiet my thought frenzy and started to drift into a calm meditation. No tears came this time, just a sudden silence from within. Once this occurred, I heard a familiar voice—though it was not near.

"You have really worked yourself up this time, lady!" It was Misty, and she seemed worried.

"My heart aches, Misty, and it's beginning to become unbearable. I am torn, thinking of my obligations here, thinking of my husband John, but unable to not think of Michael. He invades my every thought. I am so confused that I am not able to get him to convey his thoughts to me in a way that makes sense. [This action was usually an effortless action for me, a faerie gift I guess?.] He is the only one that does not fully surrender himself, and I am unable to read him. Why, Misty? Could you be wrong about him, about us?" I had to ask Misty this question because my head was in a constant spin, and my voice was filled with desperation.

"I cannot say, lady, for this is part of what you need to discover for yourself. Nila warned me that you would become distressed and your heart would begin to ache, but you must have faith in who and what you are to all of us, both human and faerie, including Michael! I can tell you this—Michael is faerie like you. Therefore, his will to resist your ability for whatever his reasons will be strong. His abilities may even match yours. They may be stronger because of his tie to the leprechaun!" Misty answered.

"Misty, I'm not sure if I can do this. I don't know if I can go on with this new found information you've have presented me with. My heart just can't take much more, and I am being tortured every single day. I can feel the familiarity of who we are together, and I so often have the urge to just run to him and shake him until he wakes up. I await his embrace and long to feel his lips against my skin. It's too often that I am hurt whenever Ciara is spoken of, and then the visual chronicles of their life appear all over the internet as if I were there with them through all of the events. It's just too much! I don't really understand who I am anymore. I'm not sure I've made the right choices in this life and I just don't know how to live! I constantly wonder if I am a failure or not because of the rules and ideas that humans have of what monetary things people should have to make them important in society. I am lost in my own skin, and I am doubting even having this conversation with you now. Actually I am very surprised I haven't been committed to a mental institution yet!" I exclaimed.

With me having said this, there was little reply from the trusted Misty. What could she say? The good-bye was suddenly lovingly conveyed, and once again, Misty's voice had disappeared. It was an abrupt exit. The most abrupt since we met. I felt even more alone. Now I felt like a terrible failure in two different dimensions! So I began to pray, speaking from my heart, and felt overwhelmed to say these words aloud, hoping that I could connect with the Great Creator once again, the way I used to when I was younger.

"Are you here with me still? Have you forgotten about me? I am unable to feel you near me. If you are speaking to me, it is like a whisper in the wind and very difficult for me to understand what it is I should do. Oh, speak to me once again I beg you, for I long to hear your voice, and I need to know you are there. I pray to you creator of heaven and earth. Help me through this time of my life."

Suddenly, I heard the most beautiful sound, a heavenly voice that seemed to surround me.

"You speak from your frail soul, my dear." This voice was different. She was resounding and comforting. I looked around and, to my surprise, was suddenly looking at what could have been one of the most beautiful figure standing before me. She was tall and statuesque with white flowing hair that seemed to float about her. Her power and beauty seemed to command the attention of the gods, but her gentleness was its own profound statement.

"Who are you, if I may be so bold to ask?" I replied.

"My name is Nila. I am the one who speaks for what is eternal, and I am here to speak to you. I feel your doubt and your anguish over this life trial put before you. Fear not, for this too shall pass, this earthly life of yours. You will find him, and he will set you free of your earthly human bonds. You cannot accomplish this task on your own, for he is the key." Nila stated.

"I think I have found him, but I am not sure. I can taste his essence in the air, and he is familiar to me. My doubt comes from circumstances, and he gives me little to feed my thoughts. It hurts, this burning fire inside of me, waiting to be unleashed. I ache inside, wanting, and needing to know if I have found my twin soul." I said.

I didn't need to explain to Nila about our circumstances, only the need to mention them. Nila knew it all already. I felt like I was sinning, doing wrong by so many people, but my situation was unique and unlike any other. I could not keep destroying the lives of people I "thought" should belong to me. Each time this happened, I knew I somehow had another strike against me. I knew that it would create a ripple effect in the many lives that were connected to me and I felt horrible.

"I hear your thoughts, dear one. The conflict within you is great. Our god does not judge you by your nature if it truly harms no one else. This is the being you are. It is within your nature to be curious—to want and be frivolous and free. You are desperate to search for what truly belongs to you. It is in your blood, it is your destiny. For this you cannot be blamed. You have paid your penance with each choice that you have made in your life throughout the years in this human world. Remember, this is how you were made to be. We understand your conflicts within, but you do not fall under the same category as the humans do. You are here in this human form to learn about the trials of their world and this dimension and to seek what it is that belongs to you to make you whole again, in order to help the faeries be whole with the humans. None can be whole without the other. You know, Titania, the universe gives us all what we need, and all we need do is ask. Humans forget to ask, it is a part of their free will. Faeries have free will too. Some souls are ready to ascend, while others tend to be suspended in time.

Now I must say this, that it must be known to you that your twin soul's true name is Khalal. Call him this when you can see that he realizes who you both are." Nila replied.

When Nila spoke Michael's faerie name, it filled me with such joy. Khalal—my true love, the one! So Michael was Khalal. Now it was just whether or not he realized who and what we both were. The waiting was the painful part.

"How much human time is wasted in wait?" I asked this of Nila with such reverence.

"You are all haunted with a deep void within. Even with the younger souls there always seems to be something missing from your lives. You expect it to be filled by a certain person, object, or project. You are desperate to fill the emptiness, but the soul tells you [if you choose to listen to it] that this void can never be filled. This is what it is to be human. You must learn to develop depth in your own invisible nature. Until your soul is free to the eternal and you return back to your faerie origins," Nila so eloquently replied, although her words gave me hope, and they frightened me as well.

What did this all mean for me and what I know as my family on this earthly plane, this life, my curiously modest existence in comparison to a faeries existence?

"You must know, Titania, of your true origins. You belong to the Ring of Fairah near Bonan, Ireland. Surely, you've felt out of place and drawn here. Think, Titania, your Gabriel is Irish! You need to keep the ties to your home there. It is said that within the faerie and the humans, heaven and earth do sleep. It lies still in the darkness. It is you who will the sweep the darkness. You have the power to will the moon to flight and the heavens with light. You are the one that has been given the charge of opening the eyes of both faerie and human alike. For to them, you are the dawn. You bring the morning. You hold back the night and give light to the skies, and the world. You are one with the one, for he has made you the dawn—queen of the faeries! Khalal is to be your king, for he is the male part of you to help rule these two worlds and mend the ties that have been broken!" Nila spoke.

"Nila, my heart is weary and tired. This world does not inspire me anymore. I feel wounded and know I do not belong here any longer. Where do I start? I can feel the faerie within me, burning and aching to be released, but I have no idea what to do. I cannot make Khalal change his mind about the earth realm. I can see that he recognizes me a little but is afraid of his own thoughts. He likes this place—he likes his human existence with Ciara." I stated.

"There is a place Titania. It is known as the Leaf's Edge, and it is near where your job is located. The location will present itself to you. Arrange a meeting with Michael there. You will see many of the faeries there, for they are all around you." Nila said.

CHAPTER 11

Self Awareness And Understanding

All at once, I could see the solution forming inside my mind; it was crazy how quickly I understood. I went to bed that night, thinking of every possible scenario, my heart pounding. Instantly I began dreaming of Michael (now known to me as Khalal).

My life continued in its normal downward spiral, thanks to Jude. Thousands of dollars were owed to people, and my life with John was slowly being destroyed until nothing monetary remained. Still I loved him so, my unwitting human guardian ever so faithful to me, not knowing the truths of his faerie queen's reality yet.

My love for John was real, but what I felt for Michael was ancient. I was beginning to understand the faerie ways. The emotions of the faeries ran deep and fierce with everything they did. This explains a lot about myself to me. It seems as though all souls are connected, and recycled, faerie or otherwise. This is why I love John so very much, he must have been with me long ago before this time. The realization of this fueled new fire in me, and I was becoming stronger in thought and emotion.

It was beginning not to matter what others thought about me. All that mattered was getting that spell broken that had been put on Michael by the leprechaun. My mind was consumed with this. It even overshadowed the evil of Jude, but this was old news in my life. I felt stronger after speaking to Nila. After all, she was the voice of God, right?

Soon I found myself having some consecutive shifts with Michael again. He seemed "normal" some days and confused and nervous the next. This made things difficult to try to plan an event after work. I spoke to another coworker about trying to do some team building, outside of the building we were trapped in for 12 hours a day. He thought it was a good idea and would mention it to the others. Michael eventually began to ask me if I would be going, and I said "Of course!" While the women of the group were busy deciding where we should have dinner and on which day, I was doing my own planning. I already knew that I somehow had to get Michael to the Leaf's Edge and that this task would be the most difficult. Nila said that certain situations would present themselves, and they began to. I just had to listen a little closer to the whispers in the wind. You see, both Michael and I were to be scheduled on morning shifts for the next month. Once the day had been decided, it was just a matter of meeting and/ or leaving together at the same time. It was not an easy task at all. So the long awaited day finally came, and I started chatting about the potential evening. Michael seemed happy but totally freaked out at the same time.

"So what do you think about the restaurant that was chosen?" I asked.

"I think it'll be okay. I heard good things about it. A buddy of mine owns it. I just have never been." Michael replied.

"Oh, cool. So you're going tonight, I guess?" I asked.

"Sure, we haven't gone out as a group in a while, so I feel like I should be there." Michael said.

"Hey, I heard some people talking about meeting up early for drinks at this place called the Leaf's Edge. It's a pub downtown. Do you think you'll be able to make that?" I asked.

"I don't know. What about you?" Michael asked.

"Well, since we both are getting off work so early, we could both change our clothes and go, right? We could leave one of our cars here and ride together if you'd like." I suggested.

As soon as my sentence had finished, Michael received a text message on his phone. Guess who? It was of course Ciara. She apparently had some issue that couldn't wait and absolutely had to speak to him about it right away at that exact moment in time. Leprechaun magic is strong. I will admit that, but on the other hand, I hadn't tapped into my own magical abilities yet! After Michael read his text message, he let out a big sigh.

"Is everything okay?" I asked?

"Yeah, I just need to do something after work." Michael said.

"Oh, okay . . . You think you're still going to be able to make it to the pub?" I asked.

"I'll try to get there as soon as I can." said Michael.

So our day went on. It was just the two of us working because it was the weekend. Soon the day came to its close. Business as usual, and it was time to leave.

"Okay, so I guess I'll see you later, right?" I asked Michael.

"Yeah, I'll be there eventually." Michael replied.

As I parked my car just up the street from the pub, I kept thinking about Michael and wondering if he would show up before the others or if he would be too scared to do so. I had changed out of my work uniform and into something cute, something not typical of what I would usually wear. I tried not to be too obvious, so I chose some nice-fitting jeans that showed off my figure. It was a warm night, so I also chose to wear a soft yellow baby-doll blouse with some six-inch high suede sandal wedges. My hair was straight that day, but I had thought it would be nice if I curled it. The ringlets almost reached down to the very bottom of my lower back. I touched up my makeup and accentuated my eyes to make my eyelashes long enough to dust a room.

I found myself in my little car, in the parking lot of the Leaf's Edge pub, alone and waiting like a pathetic little puppy hoping to see Michael. All I could do was hope that he would show up at least an hour before everyone else did. As I walked inside, I noticed there was Celtic music playing. The room was dimly lit with the look and feel of the old Ireland.

It was strangely comforting, like a coming home of sorts, and I felt in my element. There were a few people seated in various locations of the large room that held the bar area, but it was the bar for me. I noticed the bartender was a female with blond hair, and somewhat unusual looking, and she seemed to recognize me right away.

"Come and sit awhile, my lady," she said in a Gaelic accent. "What would be your pleasure this afternoon? Consider your drink on the house. May I make a suggestion?" The bartender asked in a bubbly voice.

"Sure, whatever you think is best, thanks," I replied in such an absent, preoccupied tone.

"Oh, it's not all that bad, my lady. Truly you should know that. We're all here for you, and he will be here too. Before the others get here, that is." She said in a curious statement.

"Umm, who are you?" I asked off guard.

"Oh, let's just say a loyal follower of my lady—been asked to help. Here, I'll pour you this wildflower honey wine. Not too sweet and not too bitter. It has the ability to soothe the soul, calm the mind, and break a nasty spell!" The bartender suggested.

"Break a spell, huh? Well, this is a pretty strong one you know. It's leprechaun magic!" I said.

"Yes, yes, then you've come to the right place, haven't you? You don't recognize us all yet, because your father's magic is too strong. We or I am a leprechaun. We are part of the faerie realm as well!. Some of us are loyal, and some of us are out for ourselves. There is no bigger picture for the others, just the here and the now. Trust me, lady, Misty does!" The bartender said proudly.

"Sorry, I am having a hard time believing or trusting anything or anyone right now, especially the leprechauns. No offense, I can't imagine you could understand how I could be feeling this way. Ciara, *that's her name*, to me is simply like another Jude, only worse because she has what we all need to fulfill the prophecy my supposed father speaks of. She has my twin soul, and this to her is her pot of gold. No one seems to know that without my twin soul, I am not what I could ever be apparently, for we are one. I will not be able to survive for long in either dimension. That I am sure of." I said reverently.

Then from the shadows came two more females. They were small and lovely, one with red hair and one with black. They came over to apparently greet me and offer their pledge of loyalty. I was sure it was to prove that they were around and watching. They approached me most cautiously, like unsure felines ready to run at a moment's notice. They found that I was comfortable to be near but remained guarded. They seemed to eventually feel safe within my presence.

"Drink, my lady. The dew of the vine awaits your precious lips." The girls suggested.

I then took a sip. As I drank from the beautiful oversized crystal goblet, I felt that I was drinking pure sunshine. It tasted like a fruity punch that slowly heated up as it slid down my throat. I could feel the heat of my body radiating out of me. I felt like I was glimmering. My hair felt softer and lighter, my eyes piercing and sharp. Everything was enhanced and magnified. I quite enjoyed the feeling, as I felt more and more like myself. It seemed as though about an hour had passed, and still Michael had not arrived yet. I was on my second glass of wine, drunk with the need to feel whatever it was I was feeling with every sip in that moment. I was beginning to give up on seeing Michael, and I was starting to lose my faith in the day.

Just then I felt someone tap me on my bare left shoulder. As I slowly spun around, I noticed it was Michael. He had arrived after all, and I was very pleased to finally see him, just him with no one else to interfere. He looked a little stressed but still strikingly put together. He also had on jeans with brown leather shoes. His shirt was black with long sleeves, and he smelled divine. As I turned to greet him, he seemed slightly surprised. I stood up and he briefly looked at me up and down. I don't think anyone else could have noticed the quickness of his action to take the entire picture of me in, but I most certainly did. I could always feel his gaze upon me. I used to doubt that he had any attraction to me whatsoever, but there was no denying the chemistry and pure electricity that flowed between the both of us when we were within a foot of each other.

"Wow, you look nice!" Michael remarked as he gently hugged me. "And you smell so pretty!" He added.

"Thanks. I didn't think you were going to make it. Is everything okay?" I asked as I sat down and crossed my legs.

"May I?" Michael gestured to the seat next to mine and the glass of wine I had been drinking.

"What are you drinking?" He asked.

"Oh, the house recommended it. It's lovely. Would you like to try it?" I suggested.

"Sure, I need something right now!" Michael said.

Then Michael reached for my glass, gently sipping with the utmost care, one sip, then two, then the third. He really seemed to enjoy it. He finally noticed that he had almost drunk the entire goblet and looked a bit embarrassed.

"Oh god, I am so sorry. Here, let me buy you another! Excuse me, bartender, two more of what the lady was having please." Michael asked of the bartender.

Then I began to see a slight change in him. He was more relaxed in my presence than he had been in the past. He began to look at me more, really look at me, deeper and with much more unguarded interest. He positioned his stool closer to me and began to talk about everything he could think of. As he spoke, I noticed a type of freedom in his gestures, and he kept looking at me as if he had never seen me before.

I finally had to ask. "What is it, Michael. Are you feeling okay? Is something the matter?"

"Nothing is wrong at all, Titania. I just never realized." Just then, he stopped speaking, blinking and looking away while taking another sip of the intoxicating wine.

"Realized what, Michael. Come on, it's just me, Titania remember?." I said.

"Realized what a fool I must seem to you!" said Michael.

This statement was a surprise indeed, and it caught me off guard! He felt like a fool in front of me? I always thought that was my job? I almost felt sorry for him, almost.

"Titania, I know you!" Michael stated.

"Ah, yeah, you do Michael. We work together, remember?" I asked.

"No. I mean, I really know you from somewhere. Don't ask me how or what that even means, but you are no stranger to me," Michael said so very dearly, and then with a short pause, he asked, "So do you know when everyone is due to arrive?"

"I think in about the next twenty minutes or so. Why?" I asked.

"Would you like to get out of here? I mean, go somewhere just the two of us? If you're hungry, we could have dinner together while we are out. We could go in my car and at least just get out of the immediate area so no one from work sees that we ditched them! How about Italian for dinner?" Michael suggested.

"Okay, sure, Italian sounds great." I said.

So we quickly drank up the rest of our wine and gathered our things together as fast as we could. Michael briskly took hold of my hand, and we began walking at a fast pace to his car. The thoughts in my head raced, and I began to get very nervous, because if Ciara found out, I wasn't sure that I would be ready to fight her kind of magic. She would also just be another Jude to have to deal with, and that always came with its own set of problems.

Then there was John. I could handle John usually, but this time was an unknown. How do you explain to anyone, *Oh yeah just thought I'd let you know I'm not human, I've been visited by faeries, and I'm not supposed to be married to you. I am in love with another faerie that is supposed to help me fulfill a faerie prophecy.* Yeah, not the most convincing argument for one's actions. I had to be ready for confrontation. We both had to be properly prepared for what was yet to come. Although, none of it seemed to matter as I got lost in the simple feeling of his more-than-warm hand in mine, that feeling of pure energy rushing through my hand and up my arm, straight into my heart, making it beat a little faster and a little stronger!

Michael seemed a bit more intense and focused. He wanted to get out of the pub quickly so we wouldn't run into anyone we knew. I agreed with this because it always seemed as though they were hell-bent on keeping us apart and Michael and Ciara together. No one even had a thought of my life, and my husband. It was disheartening to mean so little. Even on the rare occasions when we all would get together, they would complain when he and I sat next to each other, when we spoke, when we laughed too much and joked. All of which was so very innocent and harmless. We simply enjoyed each other's company, and both had so much in common.

There was a time last year when we all were leaving a holiday dinner. Michael suggested that he walk me to my car (which was the gentlemanly thing to do). Of course, three others from our group dutifully followed. As we walked, I held on to his arm and kept him close. We were having so much fun just talking about the evening and enjoying the night. I noticed as we reached my car that Michael did not want to leave right away. He lingered, finding things to talk to me about and reasons to be near me until his colleague literally grabbed him by the arm and said, "Come on, big guy, it's time to go now," then pulled him away from me, insisting that they had to leave! It was interesting to see the look on Michael's face that evening when our "friend" pulled him away. He looked at me with such longing and regret. It was times such as these that made me question my own sanity and my own self-worth. I asked myself that evening if I had been imagining what had just happened with Michael, the subtle hints, the strong hugs, and the look on his face when he said goodbye. What did it all mean?

This is why we had to leave without being seen! It would be less trouble this way, no explanations, no awkward moments, no pulling us away from each other. This would truly be the first time we would be alone together without supervision and judgmental eyes. This was it! It was an opportunity to reveal his true name to him, but at what moment? How would I do this? Would he respond to me at all, or would I simply just be making a fool of myself? The human doubts began to flood my mind, and I was unsure of myself once again. A faerie queen should never be unsure of herself at any given time, I am sure, but at this very moment, I was, and I was scared that he would reject me. I needed him so very much, with every cell in my body telling me so.

"I'm sorry if this seems weird, but I just couldn't stand another moment just waiting for all of them to walk through that door!" Michael was quick to point out as we arrived at his car. He opened the door for me and helped me in. Then quickly, with a smirk on his face, ran around the back to the driver's side and hopped in.

"So where will we be going?" I asked.

"I'm not sure. We just really need to get out of here." Michael said.

CHAPTER 12

The Magic Of Dreams

As I sat next to him in his car, a very familiar feeling came over me. I could feel my body beginning to ache for him. This was embarrassing and uncomfortable for me. At first, I wasn't able to pinpoint the cause of my discomfort, since it seemed to occur when I was at work with him mostly. I just thought it was a physical issue with me and quickly made myself dismiss it, but this seemed to be a very primitive human response when it came to being near him. I needed to be with him, and the closer we got, the more I ached.

There I was, wondering once again if he felt the same as I did. I wondered if men had this primal urge to mate and reproduce. I had heard somewhere in my studies that a fertile woman is able to physically respond to the pheromones of a fertile "stud" male. This is the power of evolution at its best, but it only happened when I was around him. I bet faeries are a bit more complicated when it comes to the reproduction part, since we are supposed to live a very, very long time unless there is some kind of complication or war.

The way he smelled was magnificent to me. I could bathe in him. Now—right now—was the first inclination that he too had some sort of a physical interest in me, but was it true or brought on by the faeries? Really, at this point of my life and where I was mentally, it didn't matter at all. I could tell that there was a part of me that was beginning to become worried, but the other part (the faerie in me) was longing for progress with my soul partner, my king. Still we hadn't moved from his parking spot, and

I began to wonder what was taking so long. Time just seemed to stand still when we were together. I was hoping he wasn't having second thoughts.

"Are you okay? You seem preoccupied. Is it me?" I asked.

"Do I? I'm sorry, just thinking about the future, is all. I can't seem to help it. I've always been that way, but I am glad to be going to dinner with you of course," Michael said.

"Okay, let's get going and see where we end up," I tried to add joyfully.

Michael was always good at these kinds of decisions, so naturally I went along with his idea. We ended up at a small bistro in Pacifica by the sea. The both of us had never been there, so truly it was a clean slate. No one knew anyone or anyone's spouses, and so our secret could be kept for now. Now was the time for discovery! He was the key to unlocking our inner magic, my true identity, and I longed to be the real me once again. I could feel the need and knew the time was near but always unsure if I was fooling myself or if I was doing something wrong when it came to him, or us.

There were always too many obstacles, too many people in the way, too many human rules to have to follow. These were rules that did not apply to us, rules that had been set upon us while in our human form, and I knew that we were being stifled. Everyone was always poised in judgment of me and now of my future king as well. Eventually, I would not allow this to continue. This human world would simply fall away from my existence, or we would fall away from it.

"Allow me." And so Michael stood at my side of the car, his hand extended to help me out of the vehicle.

As I took his hand, I felt the hot energy between us. I felt it run through my hand and up my arm, and for the first time, I let myself become accustomed to the feeling, opening myself up to him and letting his energy find its way into me instead of jerking away from it in fear that I had done something wrong in that moment. Surprisingly, he did not find a reason to pull away from me as well. This at least was a good beginning.

Dinner's conversation was good, and there seemed to be a lot of personal questions asked, but not once did we mention our other lives with our human counterparts or otherwise. We shared a Caesar salad and shared our dessert as well. He ordered a bottle of wine, and we drank merrily, smiling and looking into each other's familiar eyes. Amazingly, we remained sober and very curious of each other, as if we were looking at two totally different people.

Michael was very attentive, and we both were able to anticipate each other's moves. Being alone with him was strangely comfortable and easy. Being in the presence of Michael was like being home for me, and my soul was at last at ease for the moment.

"I never knew it could be like this. I must admit I am very upset with myself for not spending this time with you sooner," Michael stated.

"Do you mind if we leave this place? I feel as though I have missed out on something about you, and I'd like to find out what that something is. I really need some fresh air, you know, close to nature. It's sort of an overwhelming feeling I am having. What about you?" I asked as I kept his gaze in mine.

He said nothing really, just gave me a look of knowing what I was talking about, and we decided to enjoy the seashore just outside the bistro. He walked by my side, my arm in his as usual. As we walked in silence with each other along the dark shore, we both noticed the bright light of the moon upon the waters. It was good to be here. This was the place known well to the enlightened as the womb of Gaia herself, a place of contemplation and knowing, the place where all life was born. This was always a place for Michael and me to go to when life seemed to become too much of a burden. Being in the water or near it was a type of cleansing for us both, I in Santa Cruz, and him in Half Moon Bay. I could see that he struggled with his urges no more, and I could feel that he wanted to kiss me. However, he did not. This was a characteristically regal show of control on his part as I always, always get what I wanted.

"Michael," I said, "are you okay with this, with us here and now?"

"Of course I am. There is just a lot to think about for me," he replied.

"I know, Michael. You think of Ciara. I think of John, but unlike you with Ciara, he does not occupy every waking moment of my days. Does it not get tiring having to think of her and your lives together and having it consume you? What you should be doing for her? Tell me, Michael, do you dream?"

"I dream a lot. To be honest, I dream about you, I think, except we are both young and living somewhere else. I can never make it out really, but I know it is not here where we are right now. I was never really sure who the girl was until now, and it is a bit strange for me. What do you dream about Titania?" Michael asked.

"For many years now, I have had a dream of a boy and a man that I could never see the face of. I could only feel his familiar touch, and I knew he was a part of me somehow. Do you think we could sit, my dear, here in the sand? I would like to play a kind of game with you. Are you up for it?" I asked.

"Sure! Here, you think?" he asked sweetly.

I took off my shoes, and he did as well. I needed to feel the connection with the earth, sand, and sea. As I placed my bare feet on the ground beneath us, I felt stronger, and it looked as though he did too. There was no conversation for a while, a sort of awkward silence. He sat quite close to me, and our legs touched as he and I faced each other in the warmth of the sand dune.

"Okay, my old friend, are you ready? Hold your hands in front of you, flat palms up. I will put my hands above yours about an inch or two, and what we need to do is look into each other's eyes. The gaze must not be broken, then after some time has passed in silence, you must tell me what you have experienced, and I with you," I said to him.

He complied and did what I suggested. As I placed my hands above his, I could immediately feel energy, and this time hot and steady. I could see him. I could see through the windows of his soul, his beautiful eyes staring back into mine. I was reminded of a free and easy feeling of being a child again as Gaia's ocean song played in the background, slow and steady, and he seemed to look right through me.

At this point, he could hold back no longer, and I felt his hands softly clutch mine. I looked down at our hands and back up to him. I brought myself to my knees and gently placed myself into his lap. I put one of my hands on his shoulder and the other softy against the side of his left cheek. I took this opportunity to take a long pause and bring myself close to him and smell his neck, lightly tracing my nose against his skin. I then pulled him close to my lips as if to tell him a secret. As he drew in closer, the space between us became hot and intense. He softly pressed his lips to mine and slowly parted his mouth. I could feel the soft flutter of his tongue inside my waiting mouth, and my body became as jelly for a moment. Then as if overcoming the rapture of this first kiss, I grabbed and pulled him closer like a hungry animal. This was it! This was what I had been missing in this human life. That feeling, that missing feeling of being completely out of control and free from my human chains. There he was, my faerie companion, and we were at last intimately communicating. For the moment, I had been set free! My nonhuman partner had responded quite nicely, the way most men (no matter what species they are) would!

CHAPTER 13

A Winged Experience

I was amazed at the absolute flood of everything I was able to feel. I was enraptured by him and could feel his thoughts and emotions. It was a welcome experience. This was another ability I seemed to have as a faerie. I knew this individual's mind and soul and could feel what he was feeling. It was marvelous! He, however, did not have the same ability, but I could tell he was able to feel the environment around him. This of course included me to some degree. As he reluctantly pulled away, I didn't need to tune into my newfound ability. The surprise on his face told me all that I needed to know. The immediate air around us glowed dimly, and I felt myself become unbound by the laws of gravity. I felt as if I had stepped out of a dark box and into the light.

"What the!" Michael exclaimed. "You, you've . . . oh my god! You . . . what happened, what did you do, what are you?" Michael exclaimed in surprise.

"What do you mean? Have I done something wrong, are you freaking out about this?" I nervously asked.

"No! No! You . . . are . . . beautiful! Different, but so beautiful! I've always seen it in you but dismissed it as my imagination. If I didn't know better, I would think you went and dressed up somehow like you normally do for the Renaissance fair, but that would have been impossible. You and I haven't left each other's side. Do you know?" Michael asked, his thoughts racing through his mind faster than his words could keep up.

"Yes, I already know what it is that I am, Michael. The question is, do you know what you are?" I asked him.

"So you are a faerie?" Michael asked reluctantly.

"Yes. More than that even. Does it freak you out? I can imagine that it would. It's not as though this is something that happens every day right?" I jokingly replied.

"I don't know. It is a little different. Not something I have ever come across in my life, you know? I have heard you speak of them when we've had our funny little conversations, and I've seen movies, but nothing like this!" said Michael.

"Are you too frightened to kiss me again?" I asked him.

Michael carefully placed his hand on my lower back and softly caressed the bottom of a delicate wing. The other hand drew itself up to my right ear and traced its new shape. He seemed to know exactly what to do, I found that I needed this moment; I needed his touch in order to truly live. Faerie rules are very different from human ones; they are subtle. When Michael touched my ear and traced its form, it threw me into frenzy, for with this simple act meant that it was time for us to mate.

As we kissed passionately, I traced his ear with my right hand, finding he had changed a little as well. This was the moment I needed to speak his faerie name to him. While in the passion of our kiss, my roaming lips found his ear with my mouth, and then I softly whispered, "Khalal."

Michael gripped me painfully tight and forced me closer to him. It was as if a light had been turned on inside him. This was the kiss of the ages, never ending and seeming perfect in every way. Many thoughts pulsed through his very skin and then into mine. His passion for me was growing at a rapid pace, as mine was for him. It was truly a blessing that we had been out in the open of the seashore. If not, I fear that the room we would have been in would have burst into flame.

Then I found that Michael was becoming curious of the name that had been whispered into his ear. "Khalal" ran through his thoughts over and over again. He wanted to ask me about it, and I drew away from his grasp slowly and methodically, looking at him as my head tilted, trying to assess his well-being.

Michael then placed his strong hands on each of my arms and had me face him. I began to explain to him that he had changed like me.

"What do you mean I've changed?" Michael asked.

"Yes, Khalal, you are of the faerie realm along with me. That is one of the reasons we are drawn to each other, regardless of our human commitments and obligations." I explained.

He jumped up with tremendous grace, and we both found ourselves face-to-face. He was a magnificent sight, with his now-black hair that glimmered like starlight and his golden green eyes like my own. He was taller somehow and had the gossamer wings of a bee. My wings were that of the dragonfly with luminescent beauty. My hair was longer now (below my bottom), thick with black curls. Khalal's hair was just about shoulder length with soft wavy curls, long enough to run my hands through. His ears were beautifully shaped but much smaller than my own. At the very sight of him, I longed for him even more. The more I looked at him, the more I could see. His golden eyes had fiery specks of green, and he had a bit of regal facial hair that framed his luscious lips. The change I was seeing in him was amazing, and the change he had been witnessing in me was equally so. This was definitely an "other worldly" experience, and totally unbelievable.

I had no idea what Michael had witnessed with me. He didn't seem particularly shocked until I felt the need to stretch. Most changes were subtle with faerie glamour. Usually, the eyes become brighter, and the hair becomes longer and, in my case, darker. The skin glows as if kissed by the sun, and the ear's shape gets longer and pointier. No, it seemed to be the wings, with a span of six feet. That must have been breathtaking to look at. Michael's eyes were wide, but he seemed as though he knew all along. No matter what the soul remembers. It would be like watching a movie you haven't seen in a long time. As the movie plays you say to yourself, *oh I remember this part!*.

"My god, Titania, how did this all happen? What does this all mean? I always knew I felt something happening, and I'm not going to lie when I say you definitely lived in my fantasies, but how did you know about the faerie thing? Did you know all along? Why didn't you say something to me?" Michael asked in a confused yet curious way.

"Oh, Michael, when was I supposed to tell you? You always had some excuse handy as to why we couldn't meet outside of work, and no, I didn't always know about this. Not to this extent, that is for sure. The only thing I knew was that something had always been missing in my life or just wasn't quite right, and I knew that there was something with you and me the moment our eyes met for the first time. You simply can't understand what our roles are here and in what the faeries refer to as the Other World. All I can tell you is that there is a being that exists, and her name is Nila. She is what is known to be the voice of God. She was the one that revealed your faerie name to me. She speaks to me, Michael. She told me that we are more than two separate beings in this world and the other. You are supposed to be a part of me, Michael, and I am a part of you. We have what is known as a glamour put upon us in this world to look human to the other humans. This glamour was put upon us at our human birth by my father, Elwyn, the king of the faeries. We had to come together in a moment of passion for us both to lose the magic of the glamour and see each other in our true forms. Our human lives are a field of learning only, or so I've been told." I explained.

As I spoke to Michael, now Khalal to me, it was more difficult than I realized to reveal so much information to him. I could feel that he was overwhelmed and a bit scared. It hurt me to see and feel this conflict within him about our situation, even though it was the same conflict I had gone through myself. He needed some time to absorb the information.

"Okay, wait a minute! So we are from another world and are not even human? Am I able to change back to the way I looked as a human if I wanted to whenever I want?" Michael asked.

"I'm not sure, Khalal, I mean, Michael. I think we are able to change at will, although I am not entirely sure. Why don't you just try right now?" I asked.

"How, Titania? I have no idea what to do." asked Michael.

"Our magic seems to lie within us, like a fruitful seed. We need to call upon it and ask it to change us as we will." I said to him.

Slowly I could see Michael feeling his new spirit. His nose caught my scent, and his confused look changed. All at once, he turned toward me, the fire of passion in his eyes once again. Soon after, I found myself lifted into the air with ease. As he slowly brought me down, we kissed hard and long, and I did not want to let him go for the fear that I would never have this chance again. As my eyes opened from a dream, I noticed he had gone back to his human form. I, however, remained in my true faerie form.

"Why haven't you changed, Titania?" asked Michael.

"Because, Khalal, this is who I prefer to be, I miss being this way. This is the most complete I have felt in a long time, in this form and here with you. I just want to make sure this isn't a dream! I fear that soon I will wake, and you will be gone, and I will once again only be a human with an elaborate imagination. I think I want to be sure that I am able to change at will. Do you feel you can fade in and out of form whenever you wish?" I asked.

"I haven't thought that far ahead yet," Michael replied.

As I stood in the warm night, feeling the new me and gazing upon my faerie betrothed, I was overwhelmed. We both really needed some time to absorb our newest developments. We had discovered our interest in each other, the fact that we both were not human, and the prospect of a new life in another dimension together. I don't think a human could have dealt with this amount of information all at once, as we have been expected to do. It was fortunate we were not human at all.

Finally, there was a point in the evening that our senses began to calm down. It was as if we were both getting a hold of a wild horse and gaining control over it, although you never really have full control of the animal itself? Funny, when I was in my faerie form, I could feel everything and everyone around me, like we were all a part of each other. I don't think Michael felt the same thing though. I knew that he was still trying to make sense of his own situation and the strong bond he had with me.

I never did understand why or even how Michael could mourn his human self or life. I always felt separate from the humans even before I found out I was of the faerie realm. When Michael looked at me, I knew at once how he was feeling. There was so much confusion in his face, and I could see the doubt in his eyes. In my mind and in my heart, I was confused and bitterly hurt. How could there be confusion about me? This was almost too much to take because I loved Michael no matter which world we might be in. When I first laid eyes on him, I knew I loved him; no one needed to convince me of anything when it came to him. The only thing I ever needed convincing of was if he felt as strongly about me.

Was this the magic of the leprechaun, or did he really love her? My heart was breaking at the very thought of it, but I had to trust Nila. I had to keep my faith. I truly did believe in the Great Creator, in the power of the universe. I believed in Nila's words that were spoken to me. It's just harder when you find yourself experiencing doubt when your expectations are very different.. The humans often speak of people being in the right place at the right time, and someone once said that Michael was just ready when he met Ciara, that it was nothing more than that. But it was more than that, much more. Ciara had a plan of her own, and that plan included my king.

I had to trust that he wanted me and that the bonds we had made in the Other World and in this one were strong enough to overcome anything. I'm sure that they were.

Still there was my human guardian at home just waiting for me. He loved me; I know he did. Funny thing, here I was, the queen of all the faeries, loved by all and treasured by the Great Creator, yet my heart wept from not being loved by this one individual. This is why I am no fan of the human world. The emotions are confusing and raw. I have found this human world to be infiltrated by horrible creatures, both of them human and otherwise, not all good.

Sure some of the creatures came from my world, but at least in that world, I had unlimited power to control them. The humans are too easily influenced, and both Michael and I had been made vulnerable in this world of the humans to experience their life. This made us susceptible to anything we would encounter here on this earth plane, but now I was in the knowing of what was true. My eyes once blinded but now can see!

I was still able to feel his soft, wet lips upon my own, and how it felt to be near him once again was all that I could think about! I was overcome by the smell of him all over me, and I loved it, but I had to continue on. I decided it was time to try to tap into the magic of what was me. As faerie queen, I should be the most powerful of the faeries. It was time to pray and call out for Nila.

At my home once again, I began to look around me and notice my life and surroundings. I noticed how blessed I was to have such a patient son and the patience and kindness of my human guardian, my human husband. I was thankful for it all, but still not at all thankful for the exposure I had to Jude! Although for some reason, Jude seemed to have faded into the background of my newfound life. No longer did my every thought seem consumed by her. Now the most consuming issue of my new life was the void I felt without Michael, the void, which had been determined in the faerie realm long ago. Did he remember nothing about the faerie realm? All I knew is that I needed completion.

Chapter 14

The Inner Faerie

Michael

 I left Titania that evening, angry and confused. My life was not at all what I had worked so hard to build. What about Ciara? I loved her, didn't I? I don't know. All I am sure of is that the first time I saw Titania, I felt something that I couldn't explain. I tried with every fiber of my being to fight the thoughts I had of her and the urge to be near her, dismissing the thoughts because there was Ciara. I felt close to Titania in a way that frustrated me. She looked different tonight, not the same as she did during the day but different somehow. She smelled different, like something wild that I wanted more of and needed to have. How could I go home to Ciara? What would I say? Would things be the same? Would she notice anything? Things were different, and Titania was definitely a part of me now. I loved looking at her. She was intoxicating, and I was addicted to the need I felt for her. Kissing her was exciting and awakened something inside me that I had never felt before, and now I know. It is because I am not human. *Oh my god, how can I not be human? This is all I've ever known, and nothing to me seems right anymore.* When I began to think of Ciara, I feel only guilt and obligation, but when any thought of Titania comes to me, I suddenly feel her, and see her as if she were with me in that moment. I love her. I love Titania; this I know. She is the very breath I take, and I am complete when I am with her, and this scares me as a man or whatever it is that I am.

"Khalal," a voice called out to Michael as he pulled off the freeway toward his home. The voice was Nila's!

"Stop the car, Khalal, and step out. It is time for you to understand who and what you are. It is time for you to truly begin to grasp who Titania is and what Ciara is."

As the car came to a stop, Michael found himself near a beautiful park with several trees. It was late, and there seemed to be no people present. Michael stepped out, cautious and unsure of himself. He noticed a light mist beginning to form all around him. Something was coming..

"Khalal, always the doubtful one the most faithful to the humans. Do not doubt what Titania has shared with you, for she speaks the truth. There are many things for you to learn of and some you may not agree with." announced Nila.

"Who, may I ask, are you? Wait! You're Nila, aren't you? The being Titania spoke of, the voice of God?" Michael asked.

"Surely you would associate me with God, for we are known by many names, and I am merely a representative of the One. Your study of the human religion you grew up in teaches you very little of the One and what we represent to all. You must first have faith in the One, then in yourself, and know that by having that faith in yourself, you must have faith in Titania, for one cannot be without the other. She is held in the most high place by us and has accepted this responsibility with dignity and grace. She has made it understood that she dislikes the humans for their carelessness of the world and now faces the charge of watching over them. She cannot do this alone, for it is your love for the humans and the human world that helps her in both your charge over the two worlds and they're existence. .

"They are both earthly planes exiting in two different dimensions, for long ago, the faeries were banished from the human plane. Titania is loved by most, but not by all. There is a division within the faerie realm, and her human guardian has brought this to light sooner than we had hoped with the woman he had a previous relationship with. There is also the matter of Ciara." Nila explained.

"What do you mean the matter of Ciara? Is there something wrong, have I done something?" Michael asked.

"You have not, my boy, but your Ciara is not at all what she seems to you. She is of the faerie realm as well, but not of the same clan as you and Titania. Ciara is of the leprechaun clan, which is divided within itself. Illusive as she is, a female leprechaun, not well-known and not usually seen by human or faeies alike. She is part of the division that exists in the faerie realm and is a supporter of the dark faerie realm and not the rule of Titania.

"There is a prophecy that all of the faeries are familiar with, and Ciara has shown interest in the dark magic of the dark arts of these particular faeries. An example would be Jude, who is connected with Titania through the human John. She knew of your existence through the prophecy and of the bond between you and Titania. We are not sure if she is 100% privy of her true self. We know she has an idea, although it seems as though she is using her faerie magic that lives inside of her quite naturally. She covets many things for her own and one of these items happen to be Titania's happiness. I am sharing this with you to help you understand that Ciara was basically commissioned by Jude and your meeting was not by chance. Ciara has cast a very powerful glamour upon herself and a powerful spell over you. You must know that what you feel for Ciara is what she wants you to feel for her. She is leprechaun, and they love to collect things they think are of value to them. You, Khalal, are of great value to her. So you see, you have not done anything that would be considered wrong, but we will say that you have not paid much heed to the situation with Titania either. We understand the reasons and that you must work through your own mind in order to see what is true. We ask that you look deep within your heart to search for your truths. Take time to quiet your mind away from everyone and everything. Go into nature and breathe in its essence, allow it to live inside of you. Only then will you know the truth, my boy." Said Nila, trying to share the bits of information he could handle.

The meeting with Nila was short. It seemed as though she was there and now gone like a fleeting thought in my mind. Did I really see this being, was it my imagination? Regardless of my doubt, I know what I've seen, and I know what I've felt today and it is not the simplest thing to understand or except. Michael thought as he walked back to his car and began to drive himself home.

CHAPTER 15

The Departure

"Her sorrow is overcoming her. Look how the mist is beginning to form around where she is. A great storm will happen soon if she does not feel there is any hope. She doesn't realize how the worlds are rearranged by her yet," Misty said with great concern to Nila.

"No, she does not. The magic within her is growing stronger. Sometimes one must journey through the darkness before they are able to live in the light again. This would seem to be true for Michael as well. These are the very things our faerie queen must learn and be able to endure before she is able to rule wisely. Her ancient love and connection to Khalal is what drives her and what harms her as well. I have spoken to him, Misty. I have planted the seeds of knowledge. Now we must wait to see if they are able to grow within him still. It is now up to him to remember their love. I can tell you it transcends both worlds. He needs only to believe in her and nothing else."

MICHAEL'S DRIVE HOME

As I drove into the driveway of my home, I could see that Ciara was waiting up for me. I dreaded having to see her at all and face whatever it was that was in store waiting in that house for me. Upon walking into the house, I could smell a strong earthy scent in the air. I began to notice a dull mustard glow in the room Ciara was in. There were plants I hadn't noticed before inside the house, and I recognized them as herbs of some sort. I thought this to be rather strange.

"So where have you been?" Ciara asked accordingly.

I could see her. When Ciara spoke, I could hear a Gaelic accent and the true tone of her voice. Her hair was red and not the normal blond she had always been to me. She even appeared to be shorter than normal. She had a peculiar smile—almost devilish—and her eyes were a piecing emerald green and not their normal blue.

"I text-messaged you, Ciara, to remind you that there was an after-work get-together." Michael explained.

"Oh, well, that's very interesting, because one of your coworkers phoned here looking for you. They said you never showed up. As a matter of fact, neither did your little helper Titania." Ciara said accusingly.

"Well, not everyone was clear on where we were all supposed to meet. Several people didn't make it, and besides, Titania is not my 'little helper.' I really wish you wouldn't try so hard to make her seem less than she truly is. She is much more than you think!" Michael replied.

"So very nice to see you're protecting her! Who is she to you anyhow? She is not me. I am everything to you. We're supposed to be planning on having a baby soon, and you should not be doing this to us!" Ciara exclaimed.

At that moment, it all became clear to me. Ciara's tricks, the constant questioning, the control, the glamour, the herbs around the home that we shared—all these were part of her trying to control me. She became repulsive to me, and I had no will to continue with this ridiculous charade any longer.

"Ciara! This is not going to work, and I feel that we should consider splitting up for a while." Michael suggested.

"You will not make me leave my home! I am what you've always wanted! How dare you? Are you trying to break up with me?" Ciara asked in a frightened yet angry voice.

"Ciara, not only am I asking you to leave, but my wish is to never lay eyes on you again. Your trickery sickens me. Oh, and when you leave, which will be tonight, I want you to take everything of yours with you, including those herbs of deceit you have strategically placed around the house!" Michael stated.

"Herbs of deceit! Who have you been talking to? What is it that you think you know about anything, Michael?" Ciaria yelled out.

"I know enough! Now leave me, you tricky little creature!" Michael said in a raised voice.

"Leave you? Ha! I don't plan on leaving you, not really. I may leave this place, but I will never leave you. You will always have me on your mind! I will make sure of that! You will find yourself constantly speaking of me and how wonderful it is to be with me. What joy I have brought to your life. This is what you will want! You will have to speak of it aloud, voice your happiness to the whole world for everyone to see. Once you have done this, you will begin to see that truly all you ever really wanted was me! You will repeat this over and over until the day comes that you wish me back into your life, and I will be waiting in the shadows for it. You know you want everyone to think that your life is perfect in every way, that you are happy and have everything that everyone else could ever want! I am the only one who can make it so. I am better than anything that you could ever imagine, better than that servant of yours that you work with! I am just a wish away, my prize. All you need to do is speak the words, and I will be at your side." Ciaro proclaimed!

Her departure was faster than I anticipated as Ciaria packed up to leave, gone home to her parents or Jude's clan, wherever that was. I was just glad to be rid of her for now, but had mixed feelings of the event. What she said before her abrupt departure was strange and cryptic, but it was good to see that I still had the ability to exercise some control over my own situation. Finally, I was able to sleep without the odd feeling of having forgotten something or of being constantly watched! I figured that it must have been some sort of leprechaun etiquette, in which once you banish them from your home, they have to leave with all their possessions and never come back until they have an invitation. Everything of hers seemed to just disappear, and there was nothing left that I could see. The house was quiet and empty. There was only myself left to contemplate everything that Nila revealed to me and my time that was spent with Titania.

This was very difficult for me to understand, where I came from, what I really was. It is an ominous thought to know that you are no longer human and that you can be ruler of a place that you were taught did not exist! My life was not what I thought. The woman I had planned to spend the rest of my life with was not even human herself, and she had placed me under some sort of a spell. I really did not have any control in my life whatsoever! What was Titania's role with me? I knew that she was the queen of the faeries. I knew that I was her chosen partner; therefore, I would be her king. Still, what was it between Titania and me? If she was the faerie queen, why was she in a lower position than me in this world? Why was she in a lower position than Ciara?

Finally, Michael spun himself into sleep due to mental exhaustion, and so the next day would come regardless of whether or not Michael was ready to understand his place in the two worlds he and Titania were a part of. Time is no one's friend in the human world. It comes with a vengeance and has no mercy. It waits for no one.

CHAPTER 16

Personal Journey

All too soon, reality of the human world came back into focus. There I was Titania, trying to grasp what I was debating on, whether or not I should reveal my true self to my human husband. Suddenly my life seemed futile, and I found that I wasn't taking things as personally as I used to, I simply didn't care about the small things. Just having the knowledge that I was not human helped tremendously with trying to be human ironically, who would have thought?

There were no visits from supernatural folk for now, no interdimensional travels, just me at home, harnessing my magic. I found that I could continue to drop or add my glamour at will, so that was a good thing. I also noticed that when I became sad or depressed, it began to rain. If I was angry, thunderclouds would appear, and if I was really angry, thunder and lightning would actually hit the ground in certain places. Gabriel, my son, would laugh at this, as he seemed to understand, but John wasn't able to piece it together. John was still quite loving and watchful of me, but at times, he felt that I was slowly slipping away.

Jude, on the other hand, seemed to be running a bit scared these days. She really didn't know what to think. Who knew what plans she was trying to cook up now that she saw me growing as a total being? She could not make out what I was yet or how powerful I was. Every move she made was innate, she just seemed to have a strong feeling about me that led her to every decision she made regarding her ex husband John and his new wife Titania. Life around me was beginning to change, and it was scary and exciting all at the same time. Sometimes when I was driving home from work, I would think of what I could work on next. Should I play with the weather, or was that even an okay thing to do? Would the Great Creator think that I was abusing my power and putting the humans in danger? Would I be knocking some ecosystem out of balance or something? I don't know, but I really wanted to see what I could do, especially when it came to Jude and Ciara. With all those years of abuse from Jude, it seemed fair to give a little payback. I knew that this was the human condition that lived inside me, having this want and need for justice and payback. Maybe it was a faerie thing as well? I wasn't sure because the feeling of being a faerie was intense, each and every emotion that a human would have times ten!

I knew that my journey was not about payback or Jude, not even about Ciara. They were merely bumps in the road of the bigger picture in the plan that was already mapped out for me. I had myself to learn about, and it seemed as though I had my soul partner back. I was beginning to feel whole again, and with Michael by my side, I knew anything was possible. This new life and these gifts I had were all given to me by the One, the Great Spirit. The reality of it all was overwhelming at best. One day I woke up and found that God was real and loved me, that faeries were real, and that I was the leader of them all. It was frightening to think about what else could be real. Did that mean that the devil was real? Were demons real? Were the stories in the Bible real? My mind was swimming with so many unanswered questions. I already knew I had mortal enemies, and faerie enemies, which meant there were others with this kind of power and how would I survive that?

I had much more to worry about than Michael right now. I had to give my worries about him to the universe and have faith that if he truly loved me, he would come to me and be by my side. My faith rested in Nila's words, and that's where they must stay for now. Until then, I had to pay attention to what I could feel building up inside me—a danger unpronounced and lucid.

Sure, it was all confusing. Does Michael love me enough to never look back on his life as a human? Also, where do I begin my journey? Do I practice working on my gifts, or do I call upon my faerie brethren to help guide me, or do I sit and pray to God about my circumstance like I did when I was a child? Everything else seemed so very unimportant to me.

Even my thoughts of Michael were slowly diminishing, disappearing in the shadow of the Great One, the God I always knew. I knew what I knew about myself from Nila and Misty. Misty was a trusted faerie friend and Nila the voice of God, but never God himself. It was told to me that he prized me and considered me most important, but as one of his children, I needed to hear it from him. I was always alone and on my own growing up, there was little to no spiritual support, but I felt his fire moving inside my soul. While in my human form, I needed recognition, and now that I was a faerie, this feeling was more of a craving and a need more intense, and still his same fire burned within me. As I lived inside myself, the lucky recipient of this vessel he had given me, it was becoming clear that I needed nothing else but the recognition and guidance from the One!

It was Saturday, and I had to go to work. I knew that I was working with Michael this weekend and tried not to think about our last encounter. The thought of what he might be thinking did cross my mind for a moment, but it really did not interest me right now. A sense of peace came over me, and I was happy with myself and thankful for it all.

I woke up and got into the shower, peaceful and content. I looked upon my vigilant human husband and blessed him for his protective arms that bound me and my son to him in this human existence. I walked into my son's room and kissed his forehead as I always did and blessed his sweet heart. Having done this, the sun had risen, and several small birds sang just outside the window. It was a glorious spring morning, a bit warmer than usual.

Finally, I arrived at work, and there was Michael, sitting in his usual spot. He looked up at me, not sure what to say, but smiled and continued on with his work. Just then, it started to become cloudy and cold. After about an hour of polite small talk and work, he looked up and noticed the dramatic changes in the weather.

I thought that he was going to pretend that he and I had never had our encounter and that nothing had happened, until he spoke to me.

"Titania, you dropped out of sight from me. One day I can't stop dreaming or thinking about you, and the next you're gone. It's been weeks, and I haven't seen or talked to you. Where have you been? I wanted to call, but John . . . well, I didn't want to stir anything up with that. I really don't know what to do. I can't seem to focus. The only thing I am able to notice is you and the nature that surrounds us. I've noticed that this morning was the first nice day I've seen in a long time, and now it's gloomy again. It's you, isn't it? You're controlling the weather somehow, aren't you? It has something to do with your mood, doesn't it?" Michael kept probing.

"You have much to learn, Michael, too much in fact. What you do not comprehend is that we are what we are and that I have a station to tend to with or without you. I haven't the time to spend cauteling you through this process of learning that you are supposedly destined to rule with me. It may be that you stay behind in this human world for now. Not that you would mind that very much! I will be sure that you are well protected and looked after. This I can do for you." I replied with very little concern.

"Wait, Titania, you have no idea what transpired the night we discovered what we truly were!" Michael said.

"What transpired, my love, is of no consequence to me. I am tired of doubting myself where you are concerned. I am tired of trying to second-guess your feelings for me. You are more volatile than the weather itself, which by the way, I've found that I do control to a certain extent." I added.

I noticed Michael became silent, not his normal condescending personality he had developed in the workplace. There seemed nothing for him to say. He was acting like a child and definitely not where I needed him to be on so many levels. This saddened me because he was someone I knew for an eternity and truly loved. He was a part of me that didn't recognize where he came from. He did not want to come to me willingly, and it hurt worse than I could have ever imagined. I began to question myself once again, and what's worse, I began to question the Great Spirit. What was it that he wanted from me, and was Michael ever part of the plan?

It is never an easy thing when you begin to question your very existence, yourself, and what it is that God wants from you. Michael seemed dumbfounded the rest of the day. He always tended to fall into himself and close off from me. I saw the wall building up around him and found myself frustrated once again with his inability to make a decision where I was concerned. He was quiet and pensive, until the end of the day came and he decidedly waited for me to walk out to our cars together. This was something he hadn't done in some time. So I obliged; it was about four in the afternoon.

"Titania, why are you saying these things to me now?" Michael asked.

I knew what he was talking about immediately and seized the opportunity to explain. Michael often chose not to open up to me in such ways. This human existence had tainted his judgment of faerie ways and faerie feelings. He was completely out of touch with himself.

"Michael, I have tried all that I can to get you to come into the reality of who we are. You have done nothing but grieve your pathetic humanity and that troll your married to! I have no room to speak, as I am married to a human myself, but I had no idea you even existed or were real until I saw you, truly saw you. Once you looked into my eyes, I knew exactly who you were to me, and I knew that we belonged to each other. Therefore, I have grown intolerant of your actions and utter lack of growth in this matter where we are concerned. You were there with me when we connected with each other exposed as faeries, were you not? Do you not feel what I feel? Do you not see what I see? Does your heart not pound out of your chest and your temperature rise when we are together? Perhaps it is just I that feel this for now. You seem to have no memory of us in the Other World— what we were to each other. You worshiped me and I you. You have always been ruler of my heart, dear one. I will not deny that this doesn't pain me deeply." I answered.

"Titania, please listen to me! I am unable to remember the Other World. It all comes to me in like pieces of a dream. Nila came to me, Titania! She was magnificent! She explained about Ciara. She explained what she could about you, but it is all still very cryptic. Remember, you are married to a human. This is hard for me to wrap my head around! My religion says it's adultery—a cheat, a lie." Michael stated.

"Your human religion! Michael, we are of the faerie realm. We are not *human*! None of the human rules apply, nor do they matter to us! John is my appointed human guardian, and of course, I love him for what he is, but you! Oh, you are what makes the sun rise inside me. God would not deny anyone this! This is where you and I are on different levels. I have always been able to see deeper than you, and I feel things you could not understand. If you do rule with me, Michael, you would learn to do this as well. You would be blessed with the gifts as I am. Nila seems confident that love will be enough to get you where you need to be, but if you have no memory, not even love could help us!" I said to Michael.

"Are you telling me that you are giving up on me?" Michael asked.

"Michael, we are of the faerie realm. You must feel this blood running through you, for it is like no other! Now that you know what you are, you should be more open to this. I am not giving up. It is not of my nature to do so, but I haven't the time to spend to try and convince you of your own existence. It is you who must know this deep in your very soul. Something is coming, Michael, something very big. I can feel it creeping toward me each day. I am not sure what it is yet, all I know is that I must be prepared with or without you. Of course I would be stronger with you by my side, but if the Great Spirit wants it just to be me, then it will be just that—me and my human John. I am not standing before you pretending that I have not made mistakes in this human life. I have made many, but they have all led me here. Perhaps they were not mistakes at all but pathways to what is to come?"

As I finished my words with Michael, I could see a slow understanding come over him. He needed time, and I had none to give. He softly grabbed my hand and gently kissed the inside of my wrist. This is a sign of faerie love to the only faerie of their choice. Perhaps it was just instinct on his part to do this. I simply looked at him, my ears pointed and showing through my hair, and smiled. Before I left, I softly touched his cheek and leaned in to kiss his other cheek. I would continue to see him at our job, but who knew how long I could stay in the human realm?

I was torn between my duty as the queen of the fae and my love for Michael. I was also torn between two worlds that housed both my human husband and my one-half faerie son, Gabriel. I did not want to leave him like this, as it felt so undone and unfinished. My heart was weeping and crying out for him to follow me. The question was, would he be able to?

CHAPTER 17

The Universe Speaks

As I found myself alone and in my car on my way home, I looked up toward the sky and begged for an answer from my god. I could feel my balance shifting. Everything seemed to be moving around me. I had to pull over and get out. It turned out to be a beautiful, warm afternoon.

I was near the ocean, past my usual exit. As I walked and took in the world around me, I noticed there were no people. It was a beach near my home, and there was always someone there! The ocean was calm and glassy. I could hear nothing but the breeze and the ebbing tides. I seemed to have walked into a different time and place. The normal sea life was present, but the air was fresh and crisp. I felt at peace and remembered Genesis 1:2: "The earth was formless and void, and darkness was over the deep waters. And the spirit of God was hovering over the face of the waters." As I gazed out upon the ocean before me, I began to wonder if I was truly alone. I knew there was a great presence, but I dared not question its whereabouts, until I noticed something or someone emerging from the water, what seemed to be a human man rising from the deep, sea life teaming on either side of him, calm and reverent. I dared not move in both fear and respect for this beautiful being now approaching me.

His spirit was immediately captivating. He was the most beautiful thing I had ever seen. As he stepped upon the sand, I noticed that he was of average height, about six feet tall, with shoulder-length hair of a light golden brown that shimmered in the sunlight, soft and wavy. His handsome face was perfectly framed with a close beard and brilliantly piercing aquamarine eyes. He was not human. He was not faerie. This being was immortal beyond anything I knew, beyond Nila. He had white linens gracefully wrapped around his waist and was not wet from the water at all. His skin was a golden olive color that also shimmered in the setting sunlight. As he walked toward me, he smiled softly then stopped a foot in front of me.

We stared at each other for a while, myself in absolute amazement of the being before me!

"Fear not, my child, for I am what is all around you. I am the gateway to heaven. I have given you this heaven on earth for you to be the steward of. I am your true father. I am your friend. I am your creator and your savior—the first light of a star! Remember me and my teaching. Remember my word, for it lies deep within you like a treasure in your heart.

The humans need to imagine their earth as if it were heaven, and make it so. I have created and appointed you to lead this mission. I create what is without flaw. You were created by me for me and my purpose. You have now come to learn that you are here for me at my will, this I am telling you. You now have a good understanding of what it is to be human." said this beautiful being as he spoke.

As I fell upon my knees and bowed my head, I realized this was the Great Spirit! I then felt his hand touch my shoulder, helping me up to my feet again. At the moment he touched me, I had phased back into my faerie form. He wanted to see me as I was, as he had created me. I found that I felt as though I had mourned the time lost with him. I loved him and fell into his arms. As he lovingly embraced me the way a father would a young daughter, and suddenly I was made right.

A hundred things raced through my head to ask him: Why has my life been so hard? Why was I abused as a child and then in my marriages? Why did I have to be human? Why doesn't Michael love me and want to be with me? Just to name a few. Though none of what I thought was ever spoken, he did say this:

"Child, the answers you seek lie within. You don't need me to answer them for you. Just know that I love you and trust you more than you realize, my sweet and beautiful creature. You are blessed with the strength of a thousand angels, and my spirit lives inside of you. None shall overcome!" answered the Great Spirit of God.

And with those last words, when I opened my eyes, he was gone; however, I was still in this neutral place, still in faerie form. I felt stronger and no longer doubted myself! I stood right at the edge of the tide, bare foot, and stretched my wings for the first time. I began to exercise them, and as they fluttered, I rose to the tips of my toes. Gravity was no longer an issue. I could rise up with ease anytime I chose. I stopped, wings still outstretched, and looked around. Suddenly I fluttered them as quickly as I could and shot up straight into the sky like a bullet. I dove toward the waters and skimmed my hand along the top, viewing my reflection while I flew. Sea birds soon began to follow me, and we ascended together into the sky once again. As I rose, I spun around, happy and free, and in those moments my thoughts were of Michael. I had wished he could have shared this moment with me. I buzzed around in the sky and over the ocean for a while before I decided to come back down to the earth. As I started my decent I saw what looked like another person. I was willing to bet what I saw was not a human. What I was seeing was a faerie like me. He was not the Great Spirit, but I recognized him. This was my Faerie father King Elwyn. He looked exactly like me and I could feel his spirit. It was as if no time between us had passed. This is the faerie way. As I landed he held his arms out for me to come to him. His wings were that of a dragonfly like my own, bright and beautiful.

His peppered black and grey hair still long and thick with eyes of gold. As I landed my feet lightly touched the sand and I hesitated for a moment. I wanted to look at him for a bit, and breath in the air that surrounded him because it was filled with magic. His scent was so familiar and comforting. I could hear him in my mind, welcoming me back to the earth.

"Father I have always dreamt of this day with you. I have wished many things, and wondered more. God has put my soul at rest with my life, but I've still missed you. I am so very unsure about Khalal and if he truly belongs to me." These being the first words I remember speaking to my faerie father.

"Child, always remember you are the earth and he is the seed. One cannot be without the other. This has been so since you both were little. I knew this right away. You were inseparable and used to play day and night if I allowed it. Then it came time to give you both to the mortal world. I knew what I had to do, and yet hated having to do it. You are the most precious thing to me. I would have done anything to keep you from your pain and trials of the human world. The Great One said it was the only way. I begged him for another way because you were all I had left since your other was not able to survive your birth. Giving birth for a faerie is very difficult and most do not survive. I was there when you became pregnant with your son Gabriel your ½ faerie son. It was truly a wonder you were able to survive his birth. I was so proud of you and I still am. You have learned so much, even more than myself. The Great One holds you high up on his thrown. He trusts you Titania, he hasn't put that kind of trust in anything in a very long time. Think of this; you've had to experience the human existence as his own son did. Of course your experience was very different, but you still learned what you needed to, and experienced great sorrow and pain. Your burden is to watch this precious earth slowly be destroyed. Not even our healing ways can help it now. This is what you must carry upon your fragile shoulders. The Great One knows this! I know this my child, and so do our faerie followers." My father shared.

"I missed you father!" I exclaimed.

All I could do was look at him in awe. I didn't realize it, but we were surrounded by a golden blue light. It was our connection as father and daughter. I felt warm and safe. I was even more whole and at peace, as my life was masterfully coming together. Being with my own kind filled me up. I was energized and happy. It is an absolutely indescribable feeling being in the presence of God himself. I knew that my time in this place was coming to an end for now; this alternate dimension that I had found myself in. I wondered how I would find my way back to the human world again, and found that I had to stop for a moment once my faerie father disappeared back into the Other World. I just closed my eyes and took a deep breath. When my eyes opened I was in my car at the very same beach, but this time there were humans buzzing around, walking their dogs and talking to each other about nothing of any significance in comparison to what I now had on my plate.

CHAPTER 18

False Hope And Darkness

I've always disliked most humans, but will admit that some have the potential to be great. They're spirits were bright and some full of hope, others however seemed broken and confused. These people were most disappointing to me for I could not understand how the humans such as these could convince themselves that nothing outside of themselves existed. I have figured this much out, The Great One is not responsible for these humans belief in him, or how they choose to do it. It is a choice to believe. Like choosing to be happy or choosing to live. Most humans are confused because they are not able to see god, and the standard belief is if you can't see it therefore it does not exist. It is like love, we cannot see love only feel it. As a faerie I am able to feel love incredibly deep so much so it hurts. It is what forms my very being therefore it is difficult for me to understand when the humans are able to deny themselves of the great gift that has been given to them. I often refer to Michael stuck between the worlds of both human and faerie, not knowing how to feel as a faerie, and how it would feel to be 100% in love with me. We were deeply connected and I believe still are. The wall that Michael has put up during his time in the human world is strong and thick. Even though I am the queen of the faeries I am still not able to make someone love me if they are not ready to. It must be a choice.

I try to fool myself and tell myself that I am strong and that I can do all of this on my own. I am incredibly strong in power and mind, however having only one half of my soul weakens me. As I found myself back at work the light that lived inside of me was dimming. I was never sure if I would see Michael and if I did would he see me? Michael always acted as if nothing was wrong and this was maddening. I could not relate with the human way of thinking any longer so my tolerance for their logic was minimal. Soon I felt ready to leave this earth plane and begin my fae journey with my son Gabriel by my side in his faerie role. Gabriel was not 100% ready for what was about to come but part of me lived inside of him and I knew he would always be able to cope with whatever our lives brought.

As the days progressed when Michael spoke to me it was all in riddle. I often found that nothing he said made sense, and I longed for truth to spill out of his mouth. I feel that if I didn't work with him in the hospital and didn't have to see him, I would choose not to see him at all because of this nonsense. Soon an opportunity had presented itself and Michael and I found that we were alone. Work was over now, and we were getting ourselves ready to leave for home. It was always difficult for me to see him. It was like falling into a vortex.

"I'll walk you to your car Titania its pretty late." Michael suggested.

"Ok, sounds fine I guess?" I replied.

"I've been wanting to see you like this for a while, just the two of us away from work. I've wanted to let you know how beautiful I think you are and that I miss you. Titania, I miss you. There is a part of me that misses you so very much and the other part keeps telling me that this thing we have is wrong. I do everything I can to try and be near you, and when I am with you I don't want to let you go. I was at a point in my life when I thought I wasn't capable of falling in love or being happy. I was okay with the kind of happiness I thought I had. Now there is you and each time I see you I am overwhelmed. Titania, I think I am in love with you. I have never been in love so I don't know how it feels. You listen to me when we talk, and I can be myself around you. All I seem to think about is you."

As Michael spoke to me I was hoping for more. I could see the truth in his eyes, I could hear his voice tremble. I was able to feel what he was trying to say but I needed more. I loved Michael so much that I literally could let this earth die in peril as long as I knew he would be committed to me. This was not the kind of queen our worlds needed. Michael spoke of the parts of him that were at odds with each other regarding me but did not bother to think of the parts of me that were at odds with so much more. He did not take into consideration the responsibility of the mortal and faerie worlds and the heavy guilt involved with loving him.

All that I was willing to give up for him, to capture what it was we had in our faerie time together when we were young and in the Other World. As he stood before me pouring his heart out in a restrained emotional tirade I wanted to scream. I wanted to use all the power I held inside of me to capture him in a bubble and not let him go. I wanted to curse and torture the troll he had wasted time with and make an example of her in both worlds. So many emotions too powerful to hold on to began to rise to the surface. I knew I was stronger, I knew what I wanted to do was wrong, but I just couldn't help myself. My magic did not work on Michael, I knew that. This is why I was frustrated, although my magic did work on others regardless of who and what they were. Michael clearly was not ready for such a commitment, and he knew it. He wanted a reaction from me. He wanted me to tell him what to do next, but this is something he had to work through by himself.

I felt there was a terrible battle coming. I did not know when, or with whom. This was my own cross to bear, and I would have to do it alone with hope that the Great Spirit had made me strong enough to face my future. The future is the unknown for all of us even the faeries. I cried alone in the night. The weather was the most terrible it had been in years and no one knew it was because of me. This created so much guilt. Humans died I floods and the oceans were rocked by large earth quakes that caused tsunami's. I couldn't stop it because I didn't know how.

My heart was breaking and I was letting it happen. At this point I was barely breathing and not able to understand my own emotional tirades. Let's face it, Michael wanted to stay committed to Ciara and I was merely a flash of light to him. Maybe he was really in love with Ciara?

CHAPTER 19

Hope In Gabriel

I was ashamed of being so weak. There was a very dark force coming and I was not prepared! I felt a loneness building inside of me. All I am doing is hiding from the rest of the world. Everyone sees a smile but deep down inside I am lost. Even after meeting with god himself that human doubt still rises inside of me almost taking over. After all the happiness of two worlds depends on the silence I keep. It seems as though these worlds don't exist to me, and everything I've experienced is surreal. A phantasmagoric world of shadows and nothing more. I am no good to anything or anyone if I can not love myself first.

While in my home I studied my son. He would have to learn to protect himself somehow. For myself, being the faerie queen had its advantages. I had power over all the elements, air, earth, fire, and water, but what of my son? This could be difficult to pinpoint, due to his earthly age of 18. It was anyone's guess what his true talents would be. I knew that he had been born of earth and had the advantage of being sylph like me (born of air). So logically he could potentially have control over earth and air. This was not a bad start, but could he learn how to use his power within him quickly? I was frightened everyday knowing of the horrors we faced. I couldn't let my son see my fear or my weakness.

Gabriel was strong and fearless as an 18 year old boy should be at his age. As long as his mother remained fearless he would too. Gabriel had to be my edge over the coming darkness. It was apparent that I would not be able to face this alone, I needed more of my kind for strength and magic. I had some ideas and heard stories of four sacred gifts of the faerie realm from long ago, and I needed to acquire them somehow. The first treasure would be the stone of Fal, which would scream whenever a true king of Ireland would place his feet on it. The next is the sword of Nuada, a weapon that only inflicted mortal blows when drawn. The third is the sling shot of the sun god Lugh, that never missed a target. The last being the cauldron of Dagda from which a constant supply of food came from. These treasures are a result of the Tuatha de Dannon or Sidhe. The Sidhe were the faeries that took over Ireland after a great battle took place and were trained by four druids which bestowed these gifts to them. They have been long since lost over the years. I believe if I can acquire these four items they would be of great use to me in battle. I with my bow and arrow and Gabriel with the sling shot of the sun god Lugh. The cauldron could ensure my followers be kept well fed, and the sword of Nuada for obvious reasons. Perhaps my husband John could be strong enough to wield this weapon if taught to do so?

Gabriel was growing rapidly now, he was strong and full of vigor. He wanted to prove himself in everything that involved strength and ability. Over time it was obvious to Gabriel there was something wrong with me, and he finally got his courage up to ask me.

"Mom, there's something going on with you I know it. What is it?" Gabriel asked.

It was a particularly quiet day that any normal human family may experience. It was September, and very warm outside. Gabriel had just gotten home from school and football practice. I was cooking dinner.

"What do you mean Gabriel everything is fine. Why are you asking?" I replied.

"I'm asking because you look sad! You've looked sad for a long time now. I have never seen you this way for this long mom. So when are you going to tell me?" demanded Gabriel.

"There is a lot to say Gabriel, and I'm not sure if you're ready to hear it all, but unfortunately I have no choice but to tell you." I said.

Gabriel of course looked confused and worried.

"Sit down baby and listen closely to what I am about to tell you. You know how sometimes I leave at night and go for my late afternoon walks? Well you remember the stories I would tell you about the faeries and how you and dad would joke with me and say that I was one? I am and you are as well. It's not just a crazy story anymore Gabriel. This is why you have been feeling stronger and just different lately. You're feeling it." I began to explain.

Surprisingly Gabriel said nothing and just looked at me with some doubt and wonder.

"So what kind of powers do I have?" Gabriel joyfully asked.

This question surprised me and I went on to say, "I am not sure yet, but I can see your very strong. What power feels the strongest to you?" I eagerly asked him.

He thought for a moment and looked up at me to reply, "I have killer eye site. I can see everything in its infinitesimal detail. My hearing is pretty sharp too. Mostly, when I am outside or playing football I can hear the heartbeat of the person in front of me. My strength is unmatched and I never knew why until just now. I always thought it was my imagination but whenever I looked at you, I thought I saw wings. I kept it to myself, but I always thought you were an angel. Do you look different as a faerie?" Gabriel answered.

Gabriel always made me giggle. It was exciting to be sharing the truth with him at last, but we were both learning. I took his hand and led him into our backyard. It was easier to change forms while outside in nature. Once we were outside I closed my eyes and took three deep breaths. After the third breath I lifted my arms slightly then heard a gasp from Gabriel.

"This is what I am son. I could let you see who you really are too if you'd like?"

Gabriel's eyes widened with excitement, he trusted me more than anything. This was a definite yes. I fluttered closer toward him and put the palm of my hand on his forehead and then called out to Tuatha de Dannon. In an instant he changed into his own faerie form. His ears were pointed and his eyes an emerald green. He glowed and glistened in the warm Indian summer afternoon. He grew taller and more slender. He had much sharper features but no wings. He looked more elf than faerie, but I knew what he was! His hair was a golden brown and grew passed his shoulders flowing and wavy. This was a sort of right of passage. It was appropriate as his birthday was coming soon in October.

"You now have the ability to change into this form whenever you choose, but be warned Gabriel, if you choose to use your faerie magic to do other humans harm it will be taken from you. You must learn to align your 3 souls. This is what makes you faerie and helps complete you. I will continue to help you through this process but you must take this seriously and be committed." I said.

Gabriel ran to the nearest mirror in the house and stood in front of it for a while. It is an overwhelming thing to see yourself in such a way other than the human you've seen all your life. He was very disappointed to see that he had no wings.

"Why don't I have wings mom? Your wings are so big and shimmering" Gabriel asked.

"It's because your half sylph like me, faeries born of the air. I can't be sure what your father is exactly. Remember Gabriel, when there is magic anything can change." I explained.

I needed Gabriel to grow up quickly and get up to speed. I wanted him ready and safe. I prayed that god would protect the thing I loved most above all else.

CHAPTER 20

Confused Indecision

It is now time to begin recruiting the army I needed to fight the darkness. As the days presented to me I began to feel overwhelmed. I kept up the façade of my human life, and went to my job every day as if things were normal. I still had bills to pay and food to put on the table. I had no idea what I was doing in either world or how I was going to make things happen. I needed more guidance. I was literally just going with the flow and still felt out of control.

Seeing Michael always gave me hope. I loved him with everything that I was and more. He would come around every so often, drawn to me, wanting me, but I was so unsure and could not afford to be hurt that deeply again. Nothing in my life had ever affected me quite like he did, and this I was a slave to and did not know how to control.

Soon I found myself muddling through my simple yet demanding work days and discovered that I was running into people that were verbalizing the faerie they saw in me. This was a sign to me that these people were perhaps not human at all, just posing as human like I was. I soon figured out that they were recognizing my rank and would wait for me to give the call when the time was needed!

I thought to myself that it all made perfect sense. Of course, my subjects would come to me and that I would not need to find them, for they were all around me. There were even some humans that knew, and I would often hear that I did not walk on this earth. It was a profound statement for a human to make. I knew that a battle was coming fast because I could feel it pull at me from the inside. It felt much like a human knowing when they are about to die. Something inside them doesn't feel right; this is what prompts them to go to a doctor. Then they are diagnosed, and soon they choose to fight or die, or die fighting. Either way, the odds are fifty-fifty. Certain things come into play, key things that make the essence of a being's life: faerie faith or human faith, hope, and love. Faith in something bigger than you, hope that the idea is true and that you are forgiven and loved no matter who and what you are. Last is love. This is a tricky part of the three fates—love for yourself, respect for yourself, and having faith in yourself. These are the three keys to forever for anything that lives, including myself, for I am no different to the Great Creator. I have hopes and dreams for myself and for the humans. I must have faith that the Great Spirit will show me the way and be at my side.

I must have faith in his greatness. I must have hope that he still loves me despite all my imperfections and doubts in myself. I must continue to have hope for love itself because it is love that defines me, for I am made of the Great Spirit's love. I must have faith and hope in Michael and my love for him.

Each moment I got to spend with Michael, I couldn't help but know how much love I felt for him. However brief the time, however fleeting the glances and brushes against each other might be, I've found that it brought him closer to me somehow. I could feel him wanting to be near me like a moth to a flame. I truly never noticed this before, but now I was able to see and feel his need to be near. My human mate John was just that, human. I found myself unable to relate to him. He was a consort and a friend, but not Michael. I needed Michael. I was afraid that I would eventually injure John. The more faerie I became, the stronger my feelings were. It was harder to satisfy me in every way; I needed another faerie. I needed to be with my own species.

Don't get me wrong, John was a larger human, and he was strong, but as a faerie, we don't age the same way the humans do. We tend to stay strong. We change (look different) but not by physical deterioration. I was afraid for my human, but I would take care of him if he chose to stay my human.

I was able to see the changes in Michael. I often wondered if he saw the changes in me as well; I soon had my answer.

One day both Michael and I were scheduled to work the same shift. The exchange between us was an old familiar feeling that I hadn't felt with him in a very long time. We laughed again and were carefree as we went about our mundane workday. Then all at once, he turned and looked at me, asking why I had been angry with him.

"Titania, I have been thinking a lot about our last exchange, and you were so mad at me. Why are you nice again?" he asked.

"Mad at you? I was never mad, disappointed and frustrated, but never mad. Michael, you must understand I haven't the time to try and figure things out between you and I. Even though I would love to dedicate all of the time I had to it, I simply can't—well, I shouldn't. My mind is always preoccupied with thoughts of you. Loving you is not in my control Michael. It is what we are. Don't ask me how I know this, I just do. This knowledge pours out of me, and it's hard to know what to do with it. Without you, I am so cold inside. Nothing has ever hurt me the way you have, and that is frightening to me." I said.

Having said that, he pulled me close to him, looked deep into my eyes, and simply said, "I've missed you." As he softly pressed his lips to mine and we parted our lips to let each other in, I could feel my blood surging. We both phased immediately into our faerie forms and lost track of time. Time once again stood still, and I was complete for another moment in my life. Feeling him touch me, his hands over every part of my body, and watching him were the most incredible things to me. How could we have stayed apart from each other? How could he talk himself in and out of being with me?

In the midst of our faerie frenzy, the phone rang and drew us out of our world, and just in time too as we were about to commune with each other, not caring where we were!

As Michael took the call, I tried to fix and adjust myself. It became difficult for me to phase back into my human form more and more. It was particularly difficult keeping composure as I gazed upon his faerie form. My mind was racing with thought and speculation. I was feeling the power growing inside me, and I wanted more.

Michael and I were twin souls. The flame of our soul were split in two, and we had been unwittingly searching for each other ever since the divide. This is a terrible tragedy that had to take place in order for us to learn in this human world. I was always searching for him and was always fooled by the "picture" of love and family. This explains the three marriages and several failed relationships, but all along, I was being taught something. I was being shown the way through this human life. We both had to experience the loss of each other in order to reach our full potential as faerie royal heads of the two realms. All I knew was that there simply were not enough moments spent with him, and I would have done anything, given anything in my power to have more of them. Even after our intimate time together, I still wondered about the future.

I was watching Michael as he ended the call. Slowly, casually he walked up and said, "Now where were we?"

As my mind raced trying to think of ways to be together and comprehend the feelings that were rushing through me, they were beginning to overtake me. To my surprise, Michael suggested that we meet before work started and go for a drive. I couldn't say yes fast enough. We agreed that we would meet on a Wednesday at 10:00 a.m. I had no idea what was in store or what he had planned. As far as I knew, it was just a drive.

As I showed up at our designated meeting place, I immediately saw him standing there in front of his car, waiting for me to arrive.

Michael drove a convertible Audie It was a beautiful day, and the top was down. As I drove up and saw him leaning on the hood of his car, I was captivated by him looking so handsome in his driving clothes. I promptly parked the car, and he was immediately at my car door, helping me out. He helped me with the passenger door of his car, and we backed up. We drove and drove, laughing and talking without a care in the world, and he softly grabbed my hand.

After about an hour of chatter between us, I asked if he had a destination in mind.

"No, I don't really, but I know the road ends soon," he said.

Soon we came to the end of the road into a crossroad, the ocean directly in front of us to a vista point. We both looked at each other, and he asked if we should park in the vista. I of course replied with a prompt yes!

We sat for a while, taking in the view in front of us, amazed at where the perpetual end of the road had led us to. In my mind, I asked myself, *Is it an end of the road or a beginning of something spectacular?*

Then Michael looked at me and moved in gently for a kiss. His kiss was soft and passionate and made me want him fiercely. He pulled back, licked his lips, and said softly to me, "This is the first time I've kissed you in the morning."

My heart filled with joy, and I felt like everything was okay.

"Today is a day of firsts," he said to me. "I have never been here with anyone but myself before, and I have not experienced such a day before in my life." Michael said to me.

Michael had a tendency to verbalize what I was thinking. Being with Michael was freeing, but eventually I had to come back to my human reality of being married to John. My human time was drawing to a close so quickly, and both Michael and I knew it.

We had to end our perfect day and drive back on the road from whence we came, even though neither one of us wanted to. His affections for me were growing stronger; I could feel it. As he softly kissed me good-bye, I felt as though part of my heart had stopped beating. I was not sure of when the next time would come for us to have another perfect human experience.

While driving home, I contemplated the most recent events in my life. I found that I loved John but as a protector, and a companion. I knew why the visits from Misty and Nila had stopped. They stopped promptly after my interaction with the Great Spirit. I was directly connected to him now and received my information from him and no other—and this brought peace to me. I was stronger and ready for whatever came my way. I needed no one but Michael now to complete the journey.

Jude did not matter; Ciara did not matter, for I knew I would prevail over them. I was the faerie queen! I began to experience humans or those I thought to be human approaching me and helping me along the way. The universe served me well.

Gabriel was at home when I arrived, and I could feel him beginning to shift into a consciousness he hadn't been at before. Gabriel is my son, and I shared all my thoughts with him. I've even shared my encounters with the faerie realm. Gabriel and I spoke a lot about who and what we thought we were, and Gabriel has a good idea of what he is. He is young and his beautiful mind is so full of ideas and hope of something more than what he thought he was. We often played together when he was young with bows and arrows, pretending we were hunters. Now he's grown up and feeling what I have been feeling for years. He was ready for battle and focused. Secretly we trained together with sword and bow, I with my bow, and he with his sword.

I began to focus more myself and use whatever alone time I had to meditate. During this time, I would sometimes receive text messages from one of my human teachers. She was the only one that was the most in tune with me, and it was as though she was there in my meditation. Maricella (my human teacher) was always confirming my visions, my hopes, my fears, and she was able to calm me during my times of doubt and lack of faith.

Ever since Michael and I had our outing, we had both been feeling quite uneasy and unsettled. Michael seemed to be under the impression that it had to do with his life needing to change and the confused feelings he still felt about his wife Ciara. Michael had admitted to me at some point in the many conversations we had that he felt obligated to her but had no idea what to do about it. I knew this already but was unable to help him solve this problem. I was only able to shed light and help guide him. He still had his free will, and I was unable to interfere with that.

I could only wait patiently and keep my faith that his ancient love for me was still there and would grow inside him to a point where he was unable to deny his feelings and need to be with me, regardless of circumstances or duty to his human reality. However I was becoming done with the back and forth of another's inability to make a decision.

CHAPTER 21

Returning To The Realm

I could feel the unsettling feelings stirring deep inside me, making my heart beat faster and faster until it was about to jump out of my chest. I could not ignore this feeling any longer and felt that I needed to go deeper into a meditation. That very evening, I waited for everyone in my house to either be asleep or busy themselves with what they needed to get done, and I knew I would not be disturbed. As I centered myself by lighting a blue candle made of pure beeswax, I sat staring into the blue flame. Moments later, I felt myself being pulled by a type of magnetic force from the area between my heart and stomach. There was darkness all around me except for a spectacular display of lights that formed what seemed to be a tunnel of some sort. I let myself be taken, relaxed, and rushed through the tunnel of light.

Suddenly I found myself in the Other World, near the most beautiful gazebo-like structure in the distance. It looked as though it was comprised of ivy and white birch. It stood tall and was incredibly large—this was my father's home. This vision before me was the place of my birth, the royal house.

Unwittingly, I had opened a direct portal to the faerie world, to my home. I began to walk toward the structure that was surrounded by every tree the Great Spirit had ever created tall and strong, ancient and the biggest I had ever seen to my memory. As I approached the entrance to the royal home, I noticed two elfin guards on either side of the archway. They were tall and thin, at least nine feet tall, one with blond hair down to the middle of his back and the other with black hair of the same length. Their eyes were deep and piercing and had a pensive look to them. They both looked at me and drew their swords, which seemed to grow from what appeared to be dagger-length to the size of a large sword, and both pointed their weapons at me. I could see a figure coming toward us, glowing of a greenish gold aura. It was my father, King Elwyn. As he drew closer, I saw him wave his hand as if to say stop, and the two elves stood down in a relaxed position without a word said to either one of them. My father was very commanding and regal looking, a great warrior in his day. Nothing dared cross his path, for he had proven himself so very long ago. This was the faerie way, and soon it would be my turn to have to prove my worth to not one but two realms!

The elves did not move. I could only see them look at me as if to commit my face to memory. Once my father stood in front of me and looked at me, he simply said, "Oh, child, this will not do," and I phased into my true fae form. The elves genuflected and allowed me to pass through the threshold.

Father and I walked toward the throne room that was filled with flowers and beautiful birds with a filigree chair made up of hawthorn tree and ivy, smooth and ancient. My father sat down and asked why I had come to him.

"Father, I require the cauldron of Dagda and the other three items that come from the ancient ones before us."

"This will not be easy, child. Nothing comes easily, especially the items you are requesting. I know where you could go for council to acquire what you need, but your journey is in this world. There is a sacred place known to this realm where a great tree stands. She is very old and will test you. She will not be willing to give you these items if she has them or let you know where they might be. My only request to you is that you must bring with you my high elf Kayden. His [or he is known as] elfish name is Idhrenohtar. He will be your protector while you journey in this realm. Do not be fooled. While it is beautiful here, many enemies lurk around dark corners, most you would never expect. Trust no one, and be wise. Listen to your gut. Use your first instinct as it will serve you well here. I have gotten word that you are being tracked, so be prepared, Titania. I have something for you to use while you are here."

To my surprise, my father pulled a great bow and arrow from behind his throne, as if he had been waiting for me to arrive. The bow itself was carved of hawthorn tree like his throne, and the arrows had the finest elfish steel points and beautifully feathered tips. It was of the finest craftsmanship in both realms.

"I cannot tell you where to find the great tree, for the location of her changes. This is your journey, so you must go where you feel drawn to." My father stated to me.

Everything in this particular realm depended so heavily on instinct, faith, and utter trust in one's own divinity. It was a difficult transition to make coming from the human world. The human realm seemed too heavily dependent on others and their opinion of them. The humans were in training to learn how not to depend on others but rather to reach for the power that lived inside of them to acquire what they needed. This knowledge was not easily obtained for anyone or anything in any realm. It was easier when you were raised with this belief system already set in place.

It wasn't' long until Kayden and I were on our quest for the items I needed. I felt I needed to stop and calm my mind. Too many thoughts, too many voices were swirling in and around me. As the Other World was such a very different environment it called out to it's faerie queen. Everything was alive and whispering to me. I asked Kayden to stop and keep a watchful eye while I communed with the nature of this Other World. He simply nodded and took stance ten paces from me. Kayden and I had been on our journey for just a few hours, and it had led us to a meadow with trees scattered here and there. I chose to sit near one of the trees, looking out toward the clearing.

The land was the most beautiful I'd ever seen. It looked exactly like earth's realm but untouched. Everything seemed alive here—flowers, trees, even the running waters.

This was a place that was ancient to me. I could hear the wind whispering. As I closed my eyes, I imagined what this great tree might look like. What was she? I imagined her to be a great white oak with branches plunged into the ground to steady her great weight. The wind became a bit stronger now, and the whispers more prominent.

As I continued to look about, I noticed how nature was in perfect order with whatever the beings of this realm needed or required. If I needed a place to sleep, there would be a dwelling for me to take shelter in and be safe. The elements were alive here and listened when I spoke. Air was speaking to me now—softly caressing my skin, blowing ancient words into my ears, filling my head with the knowledge I needed to find the ancient tree being my fae father told me to seek out.

I heard footsteps coming toward me, soft and quiet. I looked up and saw Kayden standing in front of me. He was most beautiful, quite lovely to look at or rather gaze upon.

"My lady, may I speak with you?" Kayden respectfully asked.

"Of course, Kayden, I would love that!" I replied.

"Lady, I have been with your father many years and love him like my own father. I have seen you born into this realm and watched your beautiful mother breathe her last breath of magic into you. This is what dying fae mothers do. I am elf but true to faerie royalty. We are the keepers of law and order in this realm, and some, like myself, are able to keep our laws true in other realms as well. I have been appointed to watch over you since your beginning and will continue to do so until my end. May I say, lady, your king is weak, Michael! He is too human, and it sickens me. He was different when he lived here, better, stronger, even as a child. You need him to be strong. M'lady, stronger than he is now, better than he is now. He has been made weak in the human realm. We are all connected here, and I feel what you feel as I am sure if you thought about it, you could feel me as well." Kayden said.

It dawned on me that once I stopped the thoughts of my quest and focused my attention on Kayden, I felt his heart and his deepest thoughts. His thoughts were pure and full of truth. I was proud to be in his mere presence. He loved me and felt I was an intricate part of his very existence.

As I looked at him, he tilted his head and softly smiled. His rough, serious persona faded away, and I knew he belonged to me. We both were quite skilled with our bow and arrow, and now I knew why. It was because he taught me when I was young, before I had to go to the human world.

"Lady, do you realize the power you hold inside yourself? All you need to do is imagine what you wish to have, and it comes. Even the items you seek!" Kayden suggested.

This is what the wind was whispering to me; this is what I had been told all my life.

"Kayden, may I ask something of you? Can you help calm my mind? I am unable to do so when Michael is so indecisive and makes me feel as if I am of no matter. When we are not connected, I am not balanced or centered." I explained to Kayden.

Kayden then sat in front of me and put his hands out for me to put my tiny hands in his. I could feel the blue flame of the fae and green flame of the elf flow between us. The spinning motion in my head stopped, and I was able to breathe. My heart slowed, and so did everything around us. I felt a part of everything! Once he let go of my hands, we stood up and looked around. I spun and drew my bow, hitting a dark figure. It was a dark faerie that had took aim at Kayden, trying to kill him. Kayden then spun around and drew three arrows, hitting three more of them. Somehow his arrows knew where to go, around trees and through obstacles, avoiding anything that was not a threat.

One was still alive. As he lay dying, Kayden began to question him, and with a haunting calmness in the hushed tones of his voice, Kayden asked, "Are there more?"

As the dark faerie looked up through dying eyes at Kayden, he then turned to look at me and answered, "Not here, elf, but if you stay, there will be more. Leave this place, lady." Said the dark dying faerie.

This faeries voice shook with fear as he spoke to me, sorrowful and frightened of his end. I laid one hand on his heart and asked the Great Spirit to bring this faerie being peace, and with a loving look, he looked up and began to become a part of the environment around him, like a fine dust.

In Kayden's long life, never had he seen such a thing as this.

"You lady are much more than you seem. This dark faerie wanted to kill you and bring your head back as a trophy, yet you show him compassion and pray with him upon his death. If what he says is true, we must go now. I know a swifter way back to the portal you need to go through."

And so with that said, we left immediately. I don't recall ever moving so quickly. I seemed to have forgotten how to move as a fae. Kayden was ancient and knowledgeable. He seemed to be reteaching me how to be once again. I had very strong feelings for Kayden and felt drawn to him. Kayden felt like home to me.

We ran swiftly through the faerie forest realm, Kayden holding my hand, guiding me to the portal. It seemed as though our very thoughts took us where we needed to be, and there it was, the spinning vortex that got me here.

"Kayden?" I called to him, not wanting to let go of his hand, my eyes tearing up.

"My lady." I could feel his warmth, his longing to stay with me and see me through this event of my life. He held my hand tightly and did not let go!

This is the moment my life changed forever! There we both were, in my room, my husband, John, asleep on the couch. No time seemed to have passed.

I looked at Kayden, and he looked at me, gazing at each other in awe and utter amazement, realizing in that moment there was no turning back. Our lives had changed, the realms had changed, our feelings had changed!

I was stronger somehow with Kayden by my side, not afraid of the confrontation with John, not afraid of losing Michael anymore. I was no longer afraid or felt weak! I could actually see my life falling into place all in an instant, and I finally realized who I was and the power I held.

Kayden helped me up from the floor, and we were both still in our true forms, both fae and elf. Change was on the breath of the wind, and we had arrived. It mattered not what the rest of the world thought, starting with John.

CHAPTER 22

Human Homecoming

We entered the living room quietly, and we both stood over him, looking down at his sleeping human body. I softly spoke. "John, wake up. It's time for you to wake up."

He opened his eyes and only saw me at first, smiled a bit, and rubbed his eyes. Not able to see much in the low light, he squinted, looking around, and his eyes caught sight of Kayden. Startled, he jumped to his feet, yelling, "Who are you, and what are you doing in my house?" John asked nervously.

I turned on the lights and stood in front of Kayden. John could not seem to grasp what it was he was seeing.

"Why are you both in costume? I thought you went to bed. Titania, who is this guy?" John asked.

"John, sit down and listen very closely to me now. We are not in costume, and this is not a dream. For now, it is too complicated to explain, but I am not human, and neither is my friend Kayden. You must listen. There is a great change happening in your world and in the world we are from. Dangerous entities and creatures unknown to you have been summoned to kill me as I have been named faerie queen of both the faerie and earth realms. This means we can no longer be together as husband and wife in the human sense. I am not meant to be with a human any longer, and you have served your purpose in this realm. I am not sure what to do with you, John, and I haven't been for a very long time. I am sorry, but the need to be with my own kind calls to me, and I must answer!" I stated.

John sat in disbelief. I wasn't sure if he was angry or shocked or heartbroken. Maybe it was a little of everything. He kept looking at Kayden up and down and then turned to me. Finally, he spoke. "I have no idea what is going on or what you are talking about. Are you seeing this guy? How could you make up such a story?" John said dismissively.

"Look at us John, do we not seem a bit different to you?" I demanded.

Both Kayden and I looked piercingly into John's eyes, and my wings unfolded and stretched to full length for John to see. At that moment, Kayden spoke aloud.

"Behold your faerie queen!" Demanded Kayden.

As John stood up and faced me, Kayden stepped to the side and closer to John. He was very protective and was ready to strike at any moment. John seemed so small compared to Kayden, as Kayden stood at least two feet taller than John's six-foot stance.

As John looked up at him with questioning eyes, Kayden did not back away but kept looking intensely into his eyes.

"What would you like me to do with your human?" Kayden asked of me.

Kayden didn't sugarcoat his words too much. He got his point across in his own way; he never minced his words.

"No, thank you, Kayden. I believe he is too shocked to misbehave." I said to Kayden.

And Kayden took a step back. John was not doing well at this point, and I felt he needed more solid proof, but time was running out for this world, myself, and Gabriel. I turned and began to walk to Gabriel's room to wake him up, while Kayden stood and kept John where he was.

My magic was growing stronger as I regained my knowledge and self-confidence. I had control of all the elements; the very air itself was at my command. I raised my hand and waved it over Gabriel's face, and he softly awoke.

"Momma, what's wrong?" Gabriel asked.

"It is time for us to go now, son. Our time here is done, and I need to take you somewhere safe." I told Gabriel.

Gabriel understood, asked no questions, and immediately changed into his nonhuman form. It was safer this way. He was stronger and swifter; we both were. These moments were very important. Much was happening all around us, and of course, the humans had no idea. Never had Gabriel and I felt we belonged in this earth realm. Thankfully, Kayden followed. I was stronger with him, regal with him. He reminded me of who I was and respected me and my son. Kayden kept John in check. John would not question me now, nor would he dare become confrontational. So many years had passed with John and I, and he became too comfortable, therefore neglecting to respect my station.

I was realizing myself now, understanding I did not have to settle for anything or anyone. If I chose to keep a man, I could keep several. This is the faerie way, but Kayden captivated me. Michael would always be there and perhaps wake from his human fog one day, but Kayden was strong, impervious to suggestion from anything other than me.

This evening, our arrival seemed long and arduous. We had to prepare for anything to happen. I had to protect my son, for soon he would lead the royal fae army. Kayden looked around everywhere to be sure nothing had followed us through the portal. This required a keen and knowing eye, for faeries came in all shapes and sizes. We were shape-shifters and, when turned, show no mercy to each other.

Kayden had this ability for no mercy when defending the royals, and he was proud.

While Kayden searched, John sat quiet and pensive. Gabriel gathered what he knew he needed while I did the same, all the while watching over my son!

"Lady, all is well. It appears nothing has come through the portal."

As Kayden finished his sentence to me, I turned to John and said, "Now I leave you. Our time here is done. You will not remember this night, but I will come back for you if you wish." I asked John.

The realism of this statement was vague at best. This was not what I necessarily wanted, but I felt an obligation to him, for he had protected me for a number of years in this earth realm. Now it seemed I must offer him the same protection as a member of my court.

Life seemed to be changing so very rapidly, like a crumbling mountain slowly falling apart and rapidly changing, creating something new and unknown for all to see. During this time in my life, I was very sensitive to everything and everyone. Kayden seemed strong enough to understand me and the situation, for realistically, even the faerie queen needed someone to hold her and bring her peace in her stormy heart. As for Gabriel, he was young and strong, just beginning his own journey and in the forming part of his life. Nothing could penetrate Gabriel's defenses if taught well and surrounded by the right things.

I knew only one thing, and this was to get Gabriel to my father in the Other World for now until I needed him.

It was time for us to be done with this area of our lives and begin what we were made for.

Chapter 23

Patience Wears Thin

"Kayden, we must go and take Gabriel to my father!" I said.

John remained in his trance of beginning to forget the last few years of his life, and this was my choice. It would hurt less for him, and we would always be sure he was protected and cared for.

In this moment, everything was decided. Kayden turned to Gabriel and nodded. They understood each other. With this, Kayden waved his hand in front of him, and a portal appeared. The elves had this ability as keepers of the realm. The three of us stepped through and found ourselves at the edge of my father's kingdom. As we walked through, the two elves that guarded the entrance to the palace did not move. Only their eyes followed us. Gabriel walked through, proud and strong. I could see my father a short distance ahead, arms open for his grandson.

Seeing this, I knew Gabriel was safe and would want for nothing. He would receive the proper training and principles needed for the rest of his life while I could go out to complete my own dangerous mission, all the while with Kayden by my side, silent and strong!

I looked at the faeries that surrounded me and felt I needed to be alone, and so I slipped away still within the walls of the palace. While walking through the ivy-lined halls that held the ancient portraits of my family, I could feel a presence I knew. The Great Spirit was with me as I could feel his warm golden glow surrounding me. At times, in my human life, it had always been my faith that suffered most. Even in this faerie form, doubt crept in from every possible corner of the world that was myself.

As I stopped in that moment and continued to feel this warmth wash over me, I was able to be calmed, and my cup that was growing empty became full. These moments were rare, and as they came to me, I must stop and let it become a part of me once again. As I stood motionless, I could feel Kayden's hand softly cup my shoulder. Slowly I turned to look into his magical eyes, deep and wise. He was a gift from the Great Spirit, although I was not sure in what capacity, but for now, he was meant to fight by my side.

As I turned to look at Kayden, he reminded me of the items we needed for battle. The cauldron of Dagda was the first item on the list, but it was nowhere to be found. The fae forest was vast, and I was looking for a needle in a haystack. My time was running out. I knew this based on the events taking place in my life, both human and fae. How could I be so utterly consumed by Michael with everything heavily weighing on my shoulders?

"Kayden, I must go back to the human realm alone." I said.

"My lady, I'm afraid this is not possible. There is too much at stake. You cannot return alone. I will not allow this!" Kayden said.

"You, my friend, have no choice! This is my wish! I assure you if there is trouble, I will call upon you, and you will know where to be. This I must do alone." I said.

I then turned, spread my wings, and shot up into the air. As I flew, I concentrated on a portal, and in the distance through the trees, I could see the gateway into the earth realm.

Soon I found myself at my place of work at the time that Michael would be leaving to go home. As I perched myself on the rooftop, I watched and saw Michael with another human woman. She of course was helpless in his presence, and I could feel her desperate hope that he would be hers. Michael was very aware of this and liked to play the game with the human women. It was more of a sport that became a sick joke. This was a side of Michael I had not seen, and I could feel my anger grow.

Through my eyes, I saw nothing but anger for the human woman for being so ignorant and such disappointment in Michael. It was as if I did not exist and never did. All the while, I had to fight human pests. When it came to defending Michael's and my love to the unknowing humans that saw us together, one small human in particular who became infatuated with me. As I was queen of the faeries and steward of the earth realm, I was always willing to have hope for the humans I'd been charged with; however, when this small human found that I had no such interest in him, he then turned to dark forces to try to ruin me. This included my relationship with Michael.

Many days followed as Michael's behavior changed toward me, and his focus was not on the Great Spirit's plan. It is said love wins in the end, but all in an instant, as I watched the interaction between Michael and this human woman, it all became quite clear. Michael's cruelty toward me and his complete disregard made me rethink my position. This pain I'd been carrying for so long was like a pot boiling over, and I could take no more. I could not stay to watch as it was breaking my heart and hardening my soul.

I stood up, sniffed the air, and went searching for the foul-smelling evil human that had helped do this to me. I took human form and searched, then I heard my phone. I had a text message. It was the small human. I promptly texted back, asking if we could meet, and he said yes immediately. We met in front of the hospital entrance. As I approached, I could see the hope and false sense of satisfaction in his eyes. I walked him to a place where there were not many people and summoned a portal, dragging him into it with me into my world, my kingdom, my domain!

Soon the elfin guards were in sight, and I was still in my human form. They dared not stop me for surely the look in my eyes was warning enough. Slowly we walked through the halls, and this pathetic foul little human felt lucky, dare I say blessed. As I entered the palace throne room, I changed into my faerie form; Kayden was to the right near the walls. I then stopped and looked at the evil little being standing before me.

"Do not speak, human, and just listen to what I ask. If you understand me, just nod your head yes or no, but do not speak unless spoken to and expected to reply. Do you understand?" I asked.

"Yes, but—" the little human then spoke out of turn.

With a flash, Kayden was at his throat with blade in hand.

"Human, do you understand?" I asked once again and saw him nod yes. "Good." I stated, I then motioned to Kayden dismissively to remove his blade and grip and step away. Turning as I motioned to Kayden, I sat on my father's throne.

"Now, tell me, human, what have you done?" I asked.

"I have no idea what you're talking about." The little human man replied.

"Careful, human, and remember, I know when you're lying, so I will ask again, what have you done? Let me remind you that you confided in me once about the foul religion you practice and the ridiculous ideas you consider gods. I feel you have done something that you should not have, and I expect you to tell me exactly what it is, or you will find I should not be so kind or forgiving." I warned.

"I did a spell for Michael to fall in love with someone else. I prayed to my god Chongo to make this happen, and I wanted you to come to me. I wanted to punish you a bit, but not hurt you." He replied.

"Ah, not hurt me but help me?" I asked.

"Yes, I wanted you to realize he was not for you and that you and I were meant for each other. I heard you got sick?" He asked.

"Hmm, yes, I did. Do you think you could remove this spell for me?" I asked.

"Yes, I will. Are you angry with me?" He asked curiously.

"No, but I would like you to do this for me please." I stated very kindly.

Kayden's face had disbelief on it as he looked on. The human took something out of his pocket and broke it in his hand then threw it on the ground and stepped on it. He then looked up at me and said, "Okay, it's done. I told you that you needed me!"

I then stood up and walked toward him. "Now take back the spell on Michael, take back everything including your selfish wishes!" I said to him.

The evil little man looked at me, confused, and said nothing. I then motioned to Kayden to seize him firmly. As Kayden held him, I raised my hands and had ivy grow up and around him. Kayden then moved to my left side, looking down at him.

"Take back all of your words, human!" I demanded.

Out of fear, he began to pray to his god in his language.

"Take back your words, I will not ask again!" I stated.

And the ivy tightened around his wrists and abdomen.

"Okay, okay, I take back the spell on Michael, on you, on the girl he found to take your place! I take it all back." He said in a hurry.

"Then it is done?" I asked.

"Yes, it is done!" He replied.

As I looked at this evil little man, I grew angry—no, furious—at the images of Michael being cruel to me and interested in new the human woman. My wings spread and shook.

"You dare try to curse me, human, to try and control me?" I shouted.

I then ripped the talisman from his neck of his false god and stepped on it in front of him.

I then swiftly reached for Kayden's sword and sliced the human's head from his body. I watched it roll away from me about seven feet, and his body went limp as his blood poured onto the floor. While holding the sword to my side, I slowly walked over and picked his lifeless head up by his hair and stuck it on an iron stake.

"Where is your God now?" I whispered. Turning to Kayden, I then handed him his sword dripping with blood and said, "Have his tongue cut from his mouth and placed backward back into his mouth. Take his head and place it outside the gates as a warning I am not a forgiving soul when my own soul is being toyed with by an evil, selfish human. I will show no mercy as mercy was not shown to me. Now take this out of my sight. Feed the body to my griffin Quinlan!" I asked of Kayden.

Quinlan the griffin was a gift from my father in my youth. I would dream of him and feel him near me, but could never be with him unless I was in deep mediation and back in the Other World.

Not soon after the beheading took place my father came into the throne room and asked what had happened. He did not appear to be pleased.

As I explained to my father the evil things this human had done, his expression softened, and he understood.

"I cannot show mercy to whom I deem do not deserve it or are beyond saving. This human is no different from the dark faeries that hunt our family as we speak, and I cannot be weakened by the ridiculous wishes of an evil human that is too ignorant to understand anything but his own want and need!" I explained.

"No, child, you cannot, but you are not weakened. You are preoccupied. Let go of the idea of Michael and let the source carry this for you for a while." These were the wise words of my father the faerie king.

Sitting at dinner with the faeries, watching Gabriel interact, and looking at my father and how regal he was, I was still consumed by the thoughts of my actions. My heart was breaking, and I was becoming cold and hollow. In my mind, I was wondering if this was what was needed for war, the thought and feeling of not caring about anything except the moment you are in. It had been a while since I had seen Kayden, since I had given him the orders to display the head of the human I had decapitated.

It was time to sleep for me. I was very tired and consumed by a different type of fire. So I left the festivities and made the long walk alone to my chambers, all along deep in thoughts of who I was and what I'd become and what I would do.

My bed was surrounded by flowers and ivy. I changed to something white and light then lay on the bed on my side. As I turned, I noticed Kayden walking out of the shadow toward my bed. I lay watching him. Not a sound came from him, but he took my hand in his to turn my wrist over and kiss the inside of it. I watched him carefully calculate his next move, his body beginning to glow a soft green hue. I began to glow white and light blue, my wings quivering as he softly reached for my face. His face was an inch away from mine, his hand softly touching my face and his thumb tracing my lips as if to prepare them for a kiss. I then sat up to meet him upright, our lips touching, embraced in a passionate kiss.

"Why do you come to my chambers, Kayden?" I asked softly.

"A queen should not carry such heavy burdens alone. I am here. I am with you. I love you, my lady. Let me love you," he said to me as he kissed me between each word, and I was taken away by his elfin spirit.

Birds woke us in the early morning, and a knock came to the chamber doors. I looked at Kayden and said, "This is probably not good news."

"Enter." I shouted.

A male faerie opened the door carefully and said, "My lady, there is news that certain faeries learned of your actions yesterday with the human. They have seen the warning you've placed outside the palace gates and wonder if war is near. It has been rumored that it is to happen in a human weeks time and near your human home's cliff side!" This faerie stated.

"Thank you, faerie, please fetch my son and send him to the throne room." I asked politely.

"Yes, lady, right away." The faerie replied.

Kayden and I readied ourselves then met with Gabriel and my father.

Kayden and I planned that we would return to the earth realm and abandon the search for the items needed for this war. Our time had run out. We gathered as many weapons and faerie guardians as we could. Gabriel was to lead them upon my command. My father was to remain in the faerie realm to guard and protect our people. One by one, we entered into the earth realm, taking on a human form when needed and watching and waiting. Kayden took care of things while I was away looking after Michael and John. I came to our human home and spoke with John. He was a very reasonable man, and the fact that his wife was not human had settled into his skin. I explained what was about to happen and what I needed. John was willing to be one of the few humans to stand with me, or rather the only human. There was always something different about my human John, something special, as if he were chosen specifically for me by the Great Spirit, but it was Michael that was the part of my spirit. We were one spirit once, and this human existence separated what once was. This is why I disliked this place so much, disliked the humans that I now protect. These creatures were so primitive in thought and feeling, barely able to function with any kind of productivity, blinded by their own visions of themselves. They knew not of what was to come. Ignorance is bliss, and my Michael was blinded, and the humans were weak.

CHAPTER 24

The Darkness Looms

To be faerie was a fickle thing. So many thoughts, so many feelings of great intensity. To be faerie was very different from the human experience. John was a good man but with a singular purpose, now his world has become larger and his purpose along with it. Kayden, my father's most prized warrior, ancient and knowledgeable—he was mine as well. But Michael. My soul cried out for him. I might be queen of the faeries, but he was my only king. As I saw the veils crumble around me and the dark faeries come closer to their attack upon this earth, upon me, and what I hold dear, my soul still cried for Michael's help.

My son was away, preparing with Kayden and my father. I did not want any distractions, so I'd sent Kayden and Gabriel away. I was choosing to gamble on myself. I knew what I must do, and so I set out to locate Michael, all the while calling him to me from deep within. I knew he would be at work; he was one for "normal" and "routine." I trusted the universe, and I trusted what I heard the source say to me within my heart.

I arrived around the time I knew Michael would be off work and waited. I would hide no more, from him, from the world. As he walked out, he stopped when he caught sight of me. It was late evening, and I was standing in the shadows, watching as various people passed by. His eyes met mine immediately, and I whispered, "Come to me and let's talk. I will not be so careful with my words any longer, Michael. You must be prepared for what is about to come. I cannot guarantee anything about this world's safety, but I know you belong with me."

"You're always so intense, Titania. Why are you always so dramatic? I've told you many times I don't know what this is. I just know that there is a connection. Perhaps next lifetime we can figure this out." Michael said dismissively.

"Clearly you require learning things the hard way, Khalal! Allow me to enlighten you." I was in my faerie form already, and Michael in his beloved human form. We were in a secluded, quiet spot on the hospital campus, and I approached him as if to kiss. As he stood in front of me, motionless, I took his left hand and placed it near my heart but just to the upper left. This is the place in the soul where the source lives and speaks to us all. I needed the universe to help me get through to him and help him see our purpose, our spiritual promise to each other.

When Michael touched my flesh, he phased into his own faerie form, so noble and proud! I was hoping our souls would connect and he would hear the voice that spoke to me so loud and clear. I needed Michael to know the inner voice of the greater intelligence inside him.

The source spoke. "Khalal, time is not yours to waste. You have been shown a great gift. Look at yourself. She stands in front of your eyes, yet still you do not see. This blessing is what I've whispered to you all your life. You know what is true. It is up to you to do the right thing. You will not be complete without her. There is more to this life than what you know it to be. You will never be content without her in your life as you complete each other and the magic you both hold when you are together. Know that we are all a part of each other. I am the source of love and knowledge. You cannot hear me if you do not listen. I am the soft whisper in an autumn wind, the flutter of a butterfly's wings on your heart. It is time for you to surrender and know I *am*." The Great One whispered.

As I looked into Michael's face, I could see an overwhelming understanding come over him. My heart was still unsteady with doubt, for I was not infallible. I still retained human attributes and idiosyncrasies. It is difficult for all of us no matter who and what we are to simply trust in the unknown. In this case, the unknown were the actions of Michael.

I could feel Michael's energy rise, his vibration becoming stronger, clearer, and then he looked at me, seeing me, seeing us. I did not fear the darkness. I did not fear the demons. There was not much on earth or the Other World I feared. The only thing I did fear was Michael not being a part of my life. I feared the thought of never having him in my life.

There still seemed to be something about the situation with Michael that my heart was not right with. Something happened to Michael along the way, in his human journey in this life, and he was lost. He was consumed, and I could no longer feel his faerie spirit. Since the Great Spirit gave us all free will, it did not matter what the ancient prophecy stated. Michael would choose what he felt, and even though I knew Michael had love for me, he was more human than faerie in this life. This is what I must deal with, the loss of this being I adore and always will, until he is ready to come back. Unfortunately, I hadn't the time to spend on the reasons why, nor did I have the time to pray about myself. There were countless humans and fae lives at stake.

As the days passed, I was in faerie form and not hiding myself from the humans. The day was coming soon when we all must realize we needed each other—human, faerie, and animal. The humans still had no concept of what the Great Spirit had for us all, and for this hope, I was without fear, for I knew he carried my very soul for me. It was my heart that must go without. As I went about my daily business with the mundane routines of the humans and the foreboding war interdimentionally looming upon these worlds, I soon found myself alone at the beach near my home. Sitting under a tree, alone in the twilight, I contemplated our fates. Alone, feeling the fear of no hope—no army, no magic, no Michael. Although I knew my god had not forsaken me, he would come to me when the time was right. However, it did not calm my fear or the pains in my heart. The time was now. I saw in the distance from the cliff the rising of the dark faeries coming from all directions. The sky became clouded and dark, and I could see the sand rumble and beings emerging from the ground. The sea bubbled with life, and creatures of the dark began to emerge. I quickly stood and looked around, finding myself alone, not surprised, but incredibly frightened. I could feel my faerie heart beat out of my chest, and I dropped to my knees in prayer.

"Please, Great Spirit, whatever comes of this day, I ask you spare this world and help these souls find their natural spirits. May my son find his way and be happy. Take my faerie soul as payment for the horrors that await these beings. Thank you for my life. Thank you for my gifts and blessings."

Suddenly I felt a portal open and found my son Gabriel and Kayden beside me with John. In the distance, I could see the sky open up with beautiful sunlight and, through the beams, a great golden eagle. It was something so big it amazed me, and by its side was my griffin Quinlan.

Quinlan landed softly behind me, and I could feel his breath at my back. Then the golden eagle circled and landed to the right side of me, and in my left hand the bow and arrows given to me by my father king Elwyn. The eagle was the Great Spirit and sitting, it stood twelve feet tall, and as I looked to my right, a single tear fell from my eye. As we looked on, I could see more golden eagles coming from breaks in the sky. To my back, Kayden, Gabriel, John, Quinlan, and some scattered faeries gathering around us on the Cliffside. As I stood with bow and arrow in hand, I was prepared to face the darkness, because I was never alone.

The End

133

Printed in the United States
By Bookmasters